Greetings from the
Golden State

Greetings from the
Golden State

a novel

LESLIE BRENNER

Henry Holt and Company | New York

Henry Holt and Company, LLC
Publishers since 1866
115 West 18th Street
New York, New York 10011

Henry Holt® is a registered trademark of
Henry Holt and Company, LLC.

Library of Congress Cataloging-in-Publication Data
Brenner, Leslie.
Greetings from the Golden State : a novel/
Leslie Brenner.—1st ed.
p.   cm.
ISBN 0-8050-6564-4 (hb)
1. San Fernando Valley (Calif.)—Fiction.   2. Boys—Fiction.   I. Title.
PS3552.R384 T43 2001   00-033540
813'.54—dc21

Henry Holt books are available for special promotions and
premiums. For details contact: Director, Special Markets.

First Edition 2001

Designed by Kelly S. Too

Printed in the United States of America
1   3   5   7   9   10   8   6   4   2

To the memory of my father

Greetings from the
Golden State

Andrew,
A Baby Boy, Is Born

On Tuesday, November 8, 1960, two important things happened: John F. Kennedy was elected president of the United States of America, and to Fanny and Don Kelbow of Los Angeles, California, a baby boy was born. He was a beautiful baby: Andrew William Kelbow, weight seven pounds, three ounces, twenty-two inches long, with a fine smattering of soft brown hair already on his head. He was born at Cedars of Lebanon Hospital, overlooking the Hollywood Freeway to the west and Chavez Ravine, future site of Dodger Stadium and Elysian Park, to the east; he was delivered by Dr. Nathan Kruller, the esteemed OB-GYN who delivered all respectable middle-class to affluent Jewish babies in Los Angeles in that era. And though Fanny was in labor on Election Day and didn't have the privilege of casting a ballot for Kennedy and against the dread Richard Milhous Nixon, Don voted with all his heart, and then went home and sterilized their West Hollywood duplex apartment in preparation for the arrival of their new son. So that when Andrew was all cleaned up, the ink removed from his tiny foot and his cheeks aglow, and Fanny had returned from her anesthetic stupor and rejoined the land of the feeling, the Kelbows were exceedingly proud and happy and they had great hope for the future of the country.

Fanny's mother Rose came west from New York City to participate in the joyous homecoming of her first grandchild. She was singularly impressed with Don's fervency in the almost ritualistic cleaning of the apartment: he wouldn't even let Rose help. When Fanny came home, Rose kept saying, "That man certainly must love his wife and baby," and the expression on her face when she said it, the tightly pinched lips, the barely perceptible shake of the head, all this added up to imply some vague kind of warning to Fanny. "That man scrubbed the walls for you," said Rose.

Andrew was a beautiful boy with long toes and a well-shaped head; he was a good baby too. He rarely cried. Fanny, a blushing youthful twenty-four, stayed home with her angel at the duplex apartment on Willoughby Street and fed him strained peas and applesauce, she played with him as he grew, she dressed him in plaid shorts and cap, she told him nothing of the world. She clipped a little red grosgrain bow tie to his Peter Pan collar and took him in the stroller on walks around the neighborhood, telling him about the trees and the flowers and houses, withholding from him essential information about the Cold War. She showed him Bozo's Big Top on La Brea, and Pink's Hot Dogs, and the KCOP television studio at the end of Detroit Street, and she took him to Plummer Park, where old Jewish ladies gossiped on benches. She lifted her dapper, diapered little boy out of the stroller, secured him into a baby swing, and swung him, he glee-ful, she ecstatic, into the crisp, ever-blue West Hollywood sky.

Don, the energetic young lawyer, worked blindly in his office building, worked hard, courted Jerry Lewis as a client, negoti-ated record deals for Bobby Darin, flew to Vegas with contracts for a young kid named Wayne Newton, and kissed his baby in the dark of night.

When Dodger Stadium was completed and Andrew was eighteen months old, Don took him to see Sandy Koufax pitch, and it was glorious there in the new ballpark with the palm trees swaying behind the scoreboard, even if it was true that Walter O'Malley had displaced hundreds of Mexican-American fami-lies when he bought up and destroyed their houses in Chavez Ravine in order to build the stadium. O'Malley had also alien-ated an entirely different segment of the population besides, the generation of Jews who likened his tactics to those of Adolf Hitler; Echo Park became occupied France and Chavez Ravine Nazi Germany, and so these older Jews swore, painful as it was, that they would never attend a game at Dodger Stadium. While Don was aware of all this, he couldn't think of his beloved Dodgers as Nazis, nor could he deprive his firstborn son of the joys of baseball afternoons, especially when the Dodgers were involved in the most exciting pennant race that Don could remember, against the Giants of San Francisco, who, from that season on, became for Don despicable.

Andrew wanted to grow up fast, and so he did. He could never stand baby food—the little jars of strained peas or mashed bananas—and it seemed to Fanny that he moved almost directly from breast milk to lamb chops. Fanny, along with everyone else in those days, was so reliant on packaged food that it never occurred to her to mash up freshly cooked carrots or pears and call it homemade baby food; no, Gerber's in the little glass jars with the googly-eyed baby picture of Humphrey Bogart was what any modern mother was *supposed* to feed her baby. And you gave them zwieback cookies, which came in pale pink and baby blue cardboard boxes, also with the baby Bogart, when they were teething. But Andrew didn't like baby food; he spat it out. He preferred to sit in his high chair and eat scrambled eggs like any grown man, or tuna, straight from the can; of this he would remain fond into adulthood.

Rose hadn't been back to visit since she came for Andrew's birth, though Fanny sent her plenty of snapshots of the darling boy, and wrote her long letters about his progress—eating solid food, walking, talking, singing, clapping his hands. Fanny preferred to talk to her mother on the phone, which she did occasionally, but every time she did, Rose spent half the conversation complaining about how much the call must be costing (all the way across the country) and how Fanny and Don weren't made of money. Soon all of this became unsatisfying to Rose, who therefore decided to visit Fanny for Andrew's imminent birthday, despite the fact that she was mortally afraid of flying. And when Fanny telephoned her the next Sunday, Rose didn't waste any time in telling her that the Bolshoi Ballet would be in Los Angeles at the time of her visit, and perhaps, if Don would agree to baby-sit, Fanny might get tickets for the two of them to attend.

Rose flew into LAX around noon on a Monday, two weeks before Andrew's second birthday, and though Fanny wanted to take her out to dinner, Rose couldn't stand the thought of paying all that money when the food at home was just as delicious. So Fanny gave in, ran over to Bishop's to pick up some whole cut-up chicken (wasn't that oxymoronic?) to broil, Birds Eye peas frozen in butter sauce, Uncle Ben's Converted Rice, iceberg lettuce, and a package of Good Seasons Italian, for which she had a special cruet ("Pour in vinegar to vinegar line, add water to water line..."), though she was always misplacing its slimy green cap.

As Fanny was driving home, Andrew had awakened from his nap, and he was sitting in Rose's lap on the black vinyl easy chair as she read him his favorite book: *Go, Dog, Go!* "Do you like my party hat?" she was saying in her long, drawn-out, serious baby-reading tone, actually the same tone she would have used for quoting from *War and Peace*, which she had read nine times and could recite entire passages from by heart. "No, I don't like your party hat," she said in a lower, male-dog voice. Andrew liked the pictures of the trees with tops that looked like blue or red bananas, and the dogs standing on top of them wearing hats with fruit or flowers on them, but he was even more interested in the underside of Rose's arm as she held the book. Though it was October, it was warm, and Rose was wearing a sleeveless cotton shell; she was only fifty-two, but Andrew knew nothing of this; to him she was an old lady, his grandma, and the skin on the underside of her arm was loose and dry and infinitely soft.

Fanny came running up the stairs, one grocery bag under her arm and the other ripping through her clenched fist, and burst through the rattling screen door, dropping everything on the floor, ginger snaps, iceberg lettuce, cans of corn, and she turned on the TV, which took maddeningly long to warm up, telling Rose breathlessly that the president was addressing the nation about

Cuba. President Kennedy was talking as the TV warmed up, speaking tensely about a clandestine, reckless, and provocative threat to world peace, and weapons of sudden mass destruction. It turned out that photographs taken by reconnaissance planes over Cuba had been confirmed to show missiles that were determined to be offensive in nature, pointing right at the United States of America, despite the several stern warnings the president had made last month regarding the Cuban Question. Fanny was afraid to look at Rose; they were both frozen, watching the screen. The president said, in the confident and well-bred Bostonian accent that Fanny normally found supremely reassuring, "We will not prematurely or unnecessarily risk the course of worldwide nuclear war in which even the fruits of victory would be ashes in our mouth, but neither will we shrink from that risk at any time it must be faced." After that, Fanny pretty much blanked out, and soon the speech was over, and Fanny started doing things sort of mechanically—picking up lettuce, cookies, corn, picking up Andrew, who had started to cry.

Then Fanny turned to Rose, who it must be admitted had lived a marvelous life, but now felt sad for the world. Fanny said slowly, and a little quizzically, "The fruits of victory would be ashes in our mouth." When she closed her eyes, bananas and oranges turned into smoldering Cuban cigars. (The whole problem made her want to smoke, so she lit up a cigarette, and in fact proceeded to chain-smoke for the entire week, much to Rose's dismay.)

When Don came home, he sat in front of the TV and watched Walter Cronkite, who was predictably solemn about the whole thing.

Later, Rose kissed Don and Andrew good night, and when

she kissed Fanny, she said, "I'm worried that I won't see you in the morning."

The week of the Cuban Missile Crisis, the world divided itself into two camps: the alarmists and the chronic deniers.

Rose fell into the alarmist camp. To her, the fact that the crisis could have happened at all meant that things had spiraled out of control, things that human beings had no business mucking around with in the first place: smashing atoms, creating such unthinkable things as weapons of mass destruction. And once we created a monster like this, there was no telling what we would do with it because the human race was not intrinsically wise about matters of its own survival, and war was war. Didn't Napoleon, after all, let Moscow burn even though he knew it would destroy art and culture, not to mention his country's own biggest fans, the Russians? The Russians, or as she constantly had to remind herself, the Soviets (which she always pronounced "Sovi-ettes," and she thought of a chorus line of leggy, red-headed Communists at Radio City Music Hall) were near to her heart—her mother had come to America from a beautiful farm near Odessa-by-the-Sea. And though of course she and her late husband, Sydney, had been bitterly, bitterly disillusioned by Stalin, they had been, as good leftists who were active in the labor movement, *sympathetic*. Khrushchev, she didn't know about.

Rose was, however, a pragmatic alarmist. "Thank God for the Bolshoi," she said.

"What do you mean?" said Fanny.

"As long as the Bolshoi is in Los Angeles, we're safe. You don't think the Russians would bomb California with their own Bolshoi in it?"

Fanny had to admit she had a point.

For her part, Fanny was a chronic denier, but one who used the language of the alarmist. "We're ashes in Kennedy's mouth," she said. "We don't have a prayer." Although she didn't really believe this was true (if she did, then why did she keep putting off buying all the bottled water and canned goods that Rose wanted her to stock in the pantry?), she deeply *feared* that it was. "What good is bottled water if we're fried to a crisp?" she kept saying.

Of course there were political considerations, and Fanny was no dummy in recognizing this. With the elections coming up in just two weeks, and the Republicans doing their usual huffing and puffing about the Red scare, Fanny knew that Kennedy *had* to do something tough. What terrified her almost as much as the threat of nuclear extinction was the idea that Richard Nixon might be elected governor of California—for his race against Pat Brown was perilously close. "If Richard Nixon beats Governor Brown," she said, "I'm leaving California."

Fanny made dinner that night, and all the nights that followed, but she couldn't eat, which was unusual for her. "I'm nervous," she said. "I think I've lost my appetite." She divided her peas into three neat little piles. "But maybe that isn't so bad," she said, "because I could stand to lose some weight." The thought of this made her hungry again, and she had two chocolate puddings for dessert.

The Kelbow household moved about that week in a state of suspended animation. *The Manchurian Candidate* had just opened in Hollywood, but everyone forgot to see it because they had more important things to worry about. Don came home early every night, unheard of in normal times in the firm, and they alternated between the Huntley-Brinkley news on Channel 4 and Walter Cronkite on Channel 2. And at the office no one could concentrate; all talk was of the crisis. Who cared about a clause in Frank Sinatra's Reprise contract when the world might end this week?

After a couple of days, Fanny gave in and bought up quantities of canned food at Bishop's, which it turned out wasn't so easy because she wasn't the first one to think of it. They were totally sold out of Bumble Bee tuna, which upset Fanny as much as the rest, and not knowing what else to do, she bought, among other things, twelve cans of Geisha brand, chunk white, packed in oil ("Twelve?" said her mother later. "What good is twelve?") and four big jars of Best Foods mayonnaise (Hellmann's, east of the Rockies), although she couldn't imagine where she would get enough celery for that amount of tuna salad in the event of civil emergency.

On Sunday afternoon Don baby-sat while Fanny drove her mother across town to the majestically shabby Shrine Auditorium to see the Bolshoi perform. As the dancers floated across the stage in *Swan Lake* in their graceful diaphanous skirts, Rose marveled at how humans could create something so beautiful and so universal, and then contemplate weapons of mass destruction. Fanny wondered if the intermission would be soon so she could pee.

As it turned out, the crisis was resolved a week after it began—Khrushchev backed down, agreeing to dismantle the missiles. He even managed to do it sort of gracefully. All in all, Kennedy looked pretty damn good, and the next week, Richard Milhous Nixon lost the race for governor.

Fanny, Don, and Rose watched his concession speech on TV with a great measure of glee. They wouldn't have Richard Milhous Nixon to kick around anymore! Everyone agreed, including the *Los Angeles Times*, that this meant the end of his political career. While they watched, Andrew systematically pulled all Fanny's books out from the bottom shelf of the bookcase, and applied magenta and yellow Play-Doh to the covers.

Fanny threw Andrew a birthday party, complete with paper hats and M&M's and noisemakers, and Fanny's several girlfriends came with their kids, and Don invited a couple of the guys from the office, who brought their wives and kids, and Rose was thrilled, and Andrew triumphant, and by the time Fanny took Rose to the airport two days later, life was once again looking pretty swell.

One Thursday afternoon the following year, Fanny brought Andrew home from the park, put him down for a nap, turned on the TV in the dining room because she liked the noise, and unpacked the groceries. When she found the Oscar Mayer baloney in one of the bags, she opened up the plastic package and laid two slices of her favorite lunchmeat directly on the ceramic tiles of the kitchen counter. The idea was intended to bring them up to room temperature. She opened the Wonder bread, in its plastic package decorated with the festive red, yellow, and blue balloons, and took out two moist and tender slices. Then she opened the refrigerator and found the Best Foods mayonnaise and applied a thin layer to each slice of Wonder bread. If it seems as though Fanny had an obsession with brand names, it's because she did. She personified brand-name loyalty: the brands were her friends. In fact, it had almost broken her heart when she had to buy the Geisha tuna instead of Bumble Bee, and the decision to do so was completely out of character, even in the face of nuclear annihilation. But since the missile crisis was resolved without disaster, the missiles packed in crates and sent back to Russia, she was superstitiously afraid to switch back to Bumble Bee, believing that if she did so, something terrible might happen again. In the meantime, she cheered herself up with her favorite baloney sandwich for lunch.

When Andrew woke up, she scrambled him an egg, and kept one eye on the soap opera on TV as she helped him eat it. After that he was still hungry, so she went in the kitchen to open a can of the Geisha tuna. When she released the can from the electric can opener, she was shocked by what she saw: the tuna was covered with broken glass. It had been packed that way! She shrieked and threw it away, and then threw away all the other cans of Geisha tuna. Her scream made Andrew cry, so she picked him up off his booster seat and held him in her arms. And then she started crying too—because what if she hadn't noticed the broken glass and Andrew had accidentally eaten it? She would have had to rush him to the hospital, and oh, it would have been horrible—maybe it would have permanently damaged him, or even killed him! She couldn't bear the thought. After that she stuck to Bumble Bee, though thirty years later when Bumble Bee was accused of trapping dolphins in their tuna nets, she would find herself in a real moral bind, the way out of which it would be difficult to rationalize. And she kicked herself a thousand times in the intervening years because she hadn't thought of suing Geisha for the broken-glass episode.

But what happened with the tuna that Thursday afternoon in November of 1963 was really nothing compared with what the entire country suffered the following day, for on that dark day, President Kennedy was shot. After that, nothing was the same.

By early 1964 Don had settled into his career as an attorney, showing particular skill in the area of contract negotiation. He had saved enough money to buy a second car, and then a house for his small family in the San Fernando Valley. A house. The Kelbows bought a ranch-style house in Van Nuys, reddish-brown with white trim, with a swimming pool and bougainvillea in the backyard and a lovely black walnut in front, with Sylvan Park Elementary School nearby and Van Nuys High School, alma mater of Marilyn Monroe and Robert Redford (although no one knew who Robert Redford was yet) just around the corner. The Kelbows, it seemed, were hunkering down.

On moving day, Stan, a first-year associate at Don's office, and his wife, Priscilla, offered to take Andrew to the movies to get him out of the movers' way; Don and Fanny gladly accepted.

Stan and Priscilla picked up Andrew at the West Hollywood apartment and took him to Hollywood, to Grauman's Chinese Theater, to see *Mary Poppins*. This was Andrew's first movie experience. Stan paid for the tickets at the box office, and then took one of Andrew's hands in his big hand, and Priscilla took the other, and together they walked up the long red carpet toward the majestic entrance to the theater; it looked like a sparkling red-and-gold Chinese palace! They were sort of outside, underneath an elaborate canopy, and Priscilla pointed out that all over the ground were the footprints of the movie stars: here was Cary Grant, here was Ava Gardner. Of course Andrew had no idea who these names represented, but they sounded so magical, and the big footprints of the men looked so impressive, and the tiny marks from the spiked heels of Lana Turner and the triangular front of the shoe so mysterious, that Andrew was transported. Priscilla said, "You know, Andrew, it's not every little boy who gets to see his first movie at Grauman's Chinese. You must be a very special little boy indeed."

The three of them sat down in the elegant seats in the middle of the theater, and Stan explained to Andrew that it's important to count the seats and sit exactly in the middle of your row in order to enjoy the movie properly. Soon, the theater filled up, and Andrew had never seen so many children in one place in his life! The heavy red curtain parted, and on the huge luminous screen appeared the spellbinding spectacle of *Mary Poppins*.

When Andrew emerged from the dark theater into the dazzling light of day on Hollywood Boulevard, he knew, even at the tender age of three, that his life was irrevocably changed.

Pilar

Margarita Pilar Takanawa decided not to have any children because she was too ugly. She decided this on August 14, 1953, the day she married Ken Takanawa, who was not exactly himself Clark Gable. "It is not a good idea," she said to her husband. "What kind of a life would they have if they look in the mirror and scream and run away from themselves?" Ken was a gardener, a tall fat Japanese man. Margarita Pilar was twenty-three years old. She was five foot seven with blue-black hair and high mestizo cheekbones. A fine black down covered most of her body and parts of her face. Margarita Pilar Takanawa thought that Margarita was an ugly name, so she called herself "Pilar." "Please," she would say when introduced. "Call me Pilar. Margarita is so ugly." When she said "ugly" it sounded like "ogly," but her English would improve with time.

Pilar met Ken in an English as a Second Language course at Van Nuys High School's adult school. Pilar's sister Lupe warned her not to enroll in school or she would be discovered and deported. "*Basura,*" said Pilar, which means "rubbish," and she enrolled anyway, thinking all the while of Highway 1, which is the road that goes from Tijuana up across the border to San Diego and beyond, along which there are many signs on the Mexico side that say NO TIRE BASURA, meaning "Don't throw rubbish." Her sister Lupe was always throwing rubbish at her in this way just because she had the good fortune herself to marry an American citizen. But since Pilar had made the trip from Oaxaca to Tijuana, and crossed the U.S. border in the trunk of a blue Oldsmobile that caught on fire in Mexicali, she had learned to be brave in the face of flying *basura*. Therefore she enrolled in night school despite her sister's warnings.

On the first night of school Ken sat at the desk to Pilar's left. He may have been a big man, but he had a soft melodious voice that Pilar rather liked, and soon they were married.

Ken had a sweet disposition, though at times he drank too much. Scotch whiskey was what he liked, and he liked it on the rocks. When Pilar announced to him on their wedding day her reasons for not wanting children, he objected to Pilar's assessment of her looks, but agreed it might be best to remain childless.

Pilar was a cleaning lady. She went to her ladies' houses at 6:30 in the morning, before they were awake, though sometimes the husbands were making coffee before they left for the office. At these times the husbands looked like intruders in their own kitchens; Pilar was the one who belonged. She was out by 3:00. She washed clothes, ironed them, washed windows, waxed floors. There were particular brands of cleaning fluids upon which she came to depend, and she always had to remind her ladies to buy vacuum-cleaner bags. She loved children. This was the main reason her ladies loved her as much as they did, because she loved their children.

After twelve years, Pilar was one of the most sought-after cleaning ladies in the San Fernando Valley. Ken now had his own landscaping service, including a truck, a nursery, and a staff of four. They bought a yellow house on Kester Avenue in Van Nuys, just north of the barrio. By 1965 Pilar was no longer one of those cleaning ladies who had to wait for the bus; Ken bought her a wonderful car: a sky-blue 1959 Rambler American.

One of her ladies was a tiny woman who died her hair bright orange. When Pilar talked to her sister Lupe about this lady she called her "La Zanahoria," which means "the carrot" in Spanish. La Zanahoria had a tiny pinched nose that looked unnatural and the high-pitched nasal voice of an Encino housewife with nothing to do. Her house was never dirty: Pilar imagined her cleaning frantically on Sunday night so she wouldn't be embarrassed when Pilar came on Monday morning. La Zanahoria's real name was Mrs. Kelbow.

One day the sister-in-law of La Zanahoria, another Mrs. Kelbow, called The Carrot and asked her if she could recommend a cleaning lady. La Zanahoria recommended Pilar.

On Wednesday morning when Pilar showed up at the new Mrs. Kelbow's door, Pilar was expecting someone not unlike La Zanahoria. Instead she got Fanny.

Fanny was plump and she wore stretchy pants with a striped man's shirt hanging out of them. She had a mess of brown curls and a gleam in her eye. She smoked incessantly. She looked like she was up to no good.

"Mrs. Kelbow?" Pilar said when Fanny opened the door. "My name is Margarita, but you call me Pilar."

Mrs. Kelbow stuck out her hand. "Please, don't call me Mrs. Kelbow," she said, and Pilar looked at her. "Your Excellency will do."

Pilar looked startled.

"Just kidding," said Mrs. Kelbow. "Call me Fanny."

Immediately this Mrs. Kelbow was Pilar's favorite lady.

Fanny was four months pregnant when Pilar came to work for her once a week, and Andrew had just turned five.

Pilar adored Andrew right away and always brought him a butterscotch candy from her candy dish at home, as well as a pork bone for their beagle, Peanuts. But Andrew was scared of Pilar and her musty Mexican smell and her car that looked like a refrigerator, and one time when he had the flu and he had to stay home from nursery school, Pilar made him something for lunch called an enchilada and he threw it up on the kitchen floor.

So that when Little Mike was born in the spring, Pilar secretly thought of the new sweet thing as her own baby. Pilar stayed at the Kelbows' and slept on the couch for two weeks after Little Mike was born; her other ladies had to make other arrangements. She liked changing Little Mike's diapers; even the smell didn't bother her, it was so innocent and babyish, and she loved the way his head rolled around on the changing table. She loved to powder his little bottom; she loved to kiss his soft white belly and the tender back of his neck.

When the two weeks were over, Pilar was disconsolate. She packed her things into the small suitcase and walked down the brick path toward her car on the street. Andrew came running after her. "Wait!" he yelled, with a hint of desperation in his voice. "You forgot your baby!" And Pilar wished that he were right.

This Was Bliss

Andrew had to go to nursery school sometimes, and it seemed like it would be forever until his birthday. His school was called Bo Peep Nursery School, and it was far away, all the way on the other side of the high school, near that white building with the big "Q" on it on the corner, and Fanny drove him there and then left him, even though he didn't want her to go. Sometimes she would come and pick him up after school and they would go to the Dog House and sit on tall stools and eat hot dogs, and Fanny liked relish on hers and onions, but Andrew only liked mustard. When he had to stay at school he ate lunch with all the children at long tables, and sometimes they had macaroni and cheese, something Fanny never made, and the macaroni were huge and there was grainy orange cheese all over them. Sometimes he saw his cousin Amy at nursery school, and she was almost his age but exactly one month younger—a bad girl. One time when they were having macaroni and cheese she did something bad, and they made her stand in the corner, but then she started crying because there was a bumblebee in the corner too, and they made her stay there anyway and all the children were laughing at her, but really they were scared too. Andrew didn't understand what made Amy bad and him good, but he knew that it was so.

On those Saturdays when Don didn't have to work, he'd take Andrew out for the afternoon, giving Fanny a chance to take care of the baby in a state of relative peace. They'd throw a ball or attempt to fly a kite in Balboa Park, or else they'd go see a matinee, with popcorn and bonbons and even Raisinets.

Fanny didn't believe in air-conditioning, because she was afraid that Andrew (and later Little Mike) would go in the swimming pool, come in the house when he was still wet, and catch cold. Plus she loved the scorching hot weather of the San Fernando Valley, even when the temperature would reach a hundred and ten and everyone else would shut themselves up in their air-conditioned, wall-to-wall-carpeted dream homes. For her part, Fanny liked walking around the house barefoot on the hard-wood floors—which she had stained, pegged, and grooved, in the manner of something she saw in a magazine, and when the temperature rose and the dry valley heat drove everyone else indoors, she would sit outside in the shade in the backyard under the rubber tree, wearing one of Don's big old undershirts over her bathing suit, and dip herself every now and then in the pool, and then she'd sit back down, dripping, with a big glass of iced tea, and play solitaire. This was bliss. Andrew would mostly play in his sandbox, often with one of the children from the enormous Catholic family next door—the perfect inexhaustible source of playmates—and sometimes the kids would go in the water with Fanny, paddling around the shallow end on a rubber raft, or playing on the steps. Once a week, a very cute young guy came to give swimming lessons to Andrew and Karen, the daughter of Fanny's friend Ellen, who lived around the corner, but finally Fanny couldn't stand it any longer because he would throw the kids screaming into the deep end when they didn't even know how to swim yet. She and her girlfriend fired him and hired a kindly old man named Mr. Burton whom the kids much preferred. As Mr. Burton held an arm under each child at the same time, helping them float on their backs in the shallow end, Fanny and Ellen sat under the rubber tree, smoking cigarettes, drinking iced tea, and playing five hundred rummy.

In August it got hotter and hotter and smoggier and smoggier and the air wouldn't move. It sat over the valley—in fact over the whole Los Angeles basin—so heavily, so hotly, that finally it drove even Fanny indoors because she had trouble breathing, and then one day the whole thing blew up. On TV that night Fanny and Don watched as blacks rioted in Watts, an area south of downtown that Fanny didn't even know existed, touched off when the police arrested someone for drunk driving. Negroes (as African Americans were then referred to in the press) were throwing stones and bricks, smashing windows, looting, turning over cars, and setting fires, and that first night they threw a Molotov cocktail in a white man's car, then pulled him out, and beat him up. The next day the police chief said, "When you keep telling people they are unfairly treated and teach them disrespect for the law you must expect this kind of thing sooner or later." Over the weekend, the rioting kept getting worse, the National Guard came in, and no one knew what to do, except the mayor, Sam Yorty, who cleverly escaped to San Francisco. For the first time in her life, Fanny began locking her door, even while she was home. A dark layer of smoke sat over the city, and Fanny felt frightened, and guilty for being frightened.

On the phone her sister-in-law in Encino told her they were buying a gun—which Fanny thought ridiculous (she wondered momentarily if they should get one too, then censored the thought). "You'll probably shoot your foot off," she said, and she repeated the story to her girlfriend Linda who lived in Sherman Oaks.

Linda answered it with a long silence. "We bought one too," she said finally.

Fanny and Don refused, even though Pacoima, a small, predominantly black neighborhood where some rioting had also been reported, lay just north of Van Nuys. Although they were nervous and fearful, deep down they felt that in their innocence and in their righteousness—for they deplored the racism and the poverty and the hopelessness, which they were certain had caused the riots—they would be protected. That Sunday, Beatlemania in New York as the Fab Four played Shea Stadium was the human-interest story on the evening news, the irony of which was not wasted on Fanny.

The same year Andrew was old enough to start kindergarten at Sylvan Park Elementary School, the first skyscrapers started pushing their timid heads through the bedrock and up toward the heavens in a small patch of land on the other side of the hill, which is the way inhabitants of the San Fernando Valley referred to the Los Angeles basin. This patch lay just north of Twentieth Century–Fox and its backlot, which didn't yet boast the *Hello*

Dolly! sets it would construct a couple of years later, reproducing faithfully and eerily the streets of the Lower East Side of New York—all in facade. To the east of Fox, a wide boulevard was bulldozed through and paved all the way to Little Santa Monica Boulevard, and it was decided this should be called "Avenue of the Stars"; at the north end of this short majestic boulevard, still deserted because the cars didn't even yet know about it, the first two skyscrapers emerged, on either side of Avenue of the Stars. And it was decided they should be called "Gateway East" and "Gateway West," and a clever footbridge was constructed to connect them. The towers rose to an impressive height of fourteen stories each, amazing not because of their lofty altitudes, but because they were by far the tallest structures around.

And so Century City was born, and Don Kelbow, rising young attorney at Goldberg, Roth, Warner and Klein, moved along with the rest of the firm to spread out on the twelfth floor of Gateway East, with marvelous views of the smoggy basin all around. This would be the year he would make partner. One Saturday after the firm moved in, Don made French toast for his family, and after breakfast they all piled in the car and drove over the hill to see his new office. They drove over the Sepulveda pass on the brand-new stretch of the San Diego Freeway, which looked like someone had cut straight through the golden-brown hills with a gigantic carving knife.

Suddenly, Don burst out laughing.

"What is it?" said Fanny.

"Look at that bumper sticker ahead of us," said Don. He was pointing to a late-model Cadillac, powder blue. It said:

RONALD REAGAN FOR GOVERNOR

"Isn't that a scream?" said Don. Reagan, at the time, was president of the Screen Actors Guild and a B-movie star. Imagine that dope running for governor of an important state like California! Fanny and Don laughed about it all the way to Don's office, and after their tour, during which Fanny got to meet Nancy Harrison, *the lady lawyer*, who said she'd be working all afternoon (which, by the way, Don often did on Saturdays), the Kelbows piled back into the car, drove out to the beach, and had shrimp Louies and homemade potato chips in Fanny's favorite little restaurant on the Santa Monica pier.

When Andrew left the fenced-off kindergarten to go to school with the big kids, he began to notice for the first time that most of the other kids were Mexican. (Yes, in fact they were *Mexican American*, or *Chicano*, but to a six-year-old child attending school in the heart of the barrio that butted up against the middle-class white neighborhood on the other side of Victory Boulevard, they were simply "Mexican.") But this wasn't the only thing that set him apart. First of all, there was his speech impediment, for Andrew couldn't say his R's. He referred to himself as "Andwoo," and for that reason he said his real name as rarely as possible. He didn't like "Andy," because Andy was the name of the kid who lived next door, the big one with the buzz cut that made him look practically bald. Therefore, Andrew had to go to Speech Therapy twice a week, which meant he would be taken out of class and made to sit in a little room with a lady who tried to teach him impossible tricks to make the "R" sound. ("Go Rrrrrrr," she would say, "like a tigerrrrr.")

Also there was the fact that he was "gifted." "Gifted" meant that along with two other kids in his class, both of whom happened to be white (and of course "white" in this part of the San Fernando Valley meant "not Hispanic," for there were no black pupils until Andrew was in fifth grade, and then there was one, a timid intelligent boy, but he disappeared the following year), he was pulled out of class once a week, on Wednesday afternoons to be precise, to "go to Gifted." These three, along with kids from all the other grades, almost all of whom happened to be white, sat in the library, which was reserved for them on that afternoon, and played fun "creative" games while everyone else had to stay in class and practice addition and subtraction. Naturally, the rest of his peers resented him for this special treatment.

And then, if that wasn't enough, he "skipped" second grade, and so was suddenly younger than everyone in his class. Now when they lined up in height order to go to an assembly, he was always first.

All of this made for a time of great humiliation and distress in school, from which he found refuge only when the bomb-drill siren began whining at ten o'clock every Friday morning, and all the kids stopped what they were doing and dove underneath their desks, clasping their hands securely behind their heads. None of the kids stopped to wonder how their clasped hands would protect their heads if the Russians dropped a bomb on their desk; nor did the teachers ever explain to them why such a drill was necessary. No, this was routine procedure, and everyone—even the bad kids—obeyed and followed it solemnly, without question, and stayed like that until the all-clear siren sounded and the teacher told them they could come out from under the desks.

The only other fact that made school tolerable for Andrew was the extent to which his teachers adored him. And he did, if the truth be told, derive a perverse kind of pleasure from completing his assignments perfectly and from having the other kids constantly lean over surreptitiously to copy his perfect work.

Fanny had turned thirty that year. "Wow!" said Andrew as Little Mike crawled around in his diaper, at one point gnawing on Peanuts's bone, "You're so *old*!" He could never imagine ever being that old.

And now people Fanny thought of as her own age were starting to say they wouldn't trust anyone over thirty. Fanny wasn't old! And the following summer she proved it. She called a babysitter (Cindy, the teenage daughter from the enormous Catholic family next door), got in the Chevy, and drove over the hill to Don's office. First she and Don had a quick sandwich, which Don's secretary picked up for them, and then they went down the elevator to the second floor, picked up two hand-painted U.S. OUT OF VIETNAM picket signs, and joined some three hundred other concerned young lawyers, doctors, and their wives on the bridge that joined Gateway East and Gateway West. The bright bulb of a camera flashed in Fanny's eyes, leaving blue dots floating in front of her whether her eyes were opened or closed, and she knew all at once, with a little thrill of pride, that now she had her very own FBI file.

As for Andrew's taste in movies, it had evolved. Instead of the cheerful movies of his innocent baby years, *Mary Poppins* and *The Sound of Music* (though he had to admit, the part when the Nazis came was pretty scary) and *101 Dalmatians* (though he had to admit, the part with Cruella de Vil was pretty scary), he now preferred the infinitely more sophisticated James Bond movies. *Dr. No* was commendable, but Andrew favored

Goldfinger. Inside his blue denim school notebook, on sheets of lined notebook paper, Andrew made careful lists of the cast and crew of his favorite movies. Sometimes he even designed ads for imaginary movies, like *The Beauregard Dilemma.* In a careful hand, using a fine black felt-tip pen, he inscribed the names of the director, screenplay by, producer, and stars, all cramped together in capital letters like they did on the real ads; then he lettered GEORGE KENNEDY AS TIGER, and outlined this in a careful black box. There it was. It looked so much like a real movie ad that when Fanny saw it she was so astounded she showed it to Don, and they decided he had real talent in this area, though they had to admit, they weren't quite sure what area it actually was.

1968

As it turned out, the country still had Richard Milhous Nixon to
kick around. Fanny said, "If Richard Nixon is elected president
of the United States, I'm leaving the country." When it was
determined that Hubert Humphrey would be the Democratic
nominee, Fanny decided she would do her part, however small,
in defeating Nixon, so she signed up as a volunteer for the
Humphrey campaign, even though she didn't particularly like
Hubert Humphrey.

The main reason she didn't like Hubert Humphrey was that
he wasn't Bobby Kennedy, just as the main reason she didn't like
Lyndon Johnson was that he wasn't J.F.K. Johnson, in fact, she
resented for his entire administration, starting with the fact that
he didn't even have the decency to wait until Air Force One
landed to be sworn in—she was sure he had something to do
with the assassination. With Bobby Kennedy, it was déjà vu all
over again, except that instead of Dallas it was her beloved
Los Angeles; and if she was distraught when J.F.K. was killed,

this time she was devastated. The day it happened she went to Sherman Oaks to get her hair cut and frosted on Ventura Boulevard, and the guy who cut it (whose name was Guy) was so upset that he accidentally gave her a crew cut the color of American cheese.

One day, Fanny was going door-to-door in Pacoima as part of the get-out-the-vote effort, and of course she had two-year-old Little Mike with her. Don thought Fanny's involvement was just terrific. She went up and down the treeless tidy streets, with their neat but shabby houses, knocking on doors, and she couldn't understand why there were so many Cadillacs and Lincolns in the driveways of such poor houses. But the important thing was, it wasn't difficult to convince the black inhabitants of this neighborhood, who struck Fanny for the most part as regular, nice middle-class people, to vote for Hubert Humphrey; it seemed they all liked him anyway.

They got to one door, that of a medium-size yellow house with white trim of which Fanny approved, with a Dodge in the driveway, about to pull out. Fanny looked at the driveway and shrieked at the top of her lungs. The car stopped, and she dashed over and scooped up the toddler that was playing with a toy truck just behind the car, which had stopped maybe a foot away; it clearly would have run over the child had Fanny not screamed. As Fanny swooped up the toddler in her arms, a middle-aged heavy-set black man jumped out of the car, and when he saw what had almost happened, he let out a little cry and took the child from Fanny, who was about to drop him anyway. The toddler's mother came running out and whooshed them all toward the house, squeezing the toddler, who looked baffled by the whole affair. "It's awfully hot out here," she said, which was true, for it was late September in Southern California. "Come on in and have some lemonade. I'll never be able to thank you enough." Fanny took Little Mike out of his stroller, which in those days were huge clunky affairs with lots of metal, and she ushered him into the yellow house; the father was weeping and couldn't seem to stop. Little Mike looked around, appearing confused, and then pronounced definitively: "It smells like pee-pee in here." Everyone was shocked for a moment, then Fanny mumbled some excuse about how he probably wet his pants, and awkwardly got the hell out of there.

Buzzy

One summer, Andrew wanted to change his name to Buzz. On July 20, 1969, *Apollo 11* landed on the moon, and Fanny and Don let the kids stay up late to watch Neil Armstrong and Buzz Aldrin do their moonwalk. "My name is Andrew," he'd practiced saying in front of the mirror. "But my friends call me 'Buzz.'" The whole thing backfired, however, when everyone started calling him Buzzy. Andrew saw *2001: A Space Odyssey* seventeen times, and almost got into a fistfight with his friend Jason, who said that *Planet of the Apes* was better and that Andrew was an idiot for thinking that the obelisk in the beginning of *2001* was supposed to represent God.

This was the summer before he was in fifth grade. In 2001 Andrew would be forty-one years old. Forty-one—no way, José!

In August, Sharon Tate was killed in some kind of ritual cult murder and it seemed this was the only thing anyone could talk about. Did it have anything to do with *Rosemary's Baby*, which Tate's husband, Roman Polanski, had just directed? Fanny became morbidly obsessed by the whole thing, and even drove by the house in Laurel Canyon where it happened. She was overcome by a dizzying feeling of gloom when she passed it. When she got home, Little Mike was doing a dance called "The Moonwalk," which he had apparently learned from the TV.

"Do you realize," said Fanny, "that we've put a man on the moon, and in Liechtenstein women still don't even have the vote?"

"Europe is a backward land," said Don. "Let's go there." And so Don, with the help of his secretary, planned a trip to Europe for his young family for October. He would have to take Andrew out of school for a month, but that was sensible, he figured, since a month in Europe—Buckingham Palace, the Louvre, the Roman Coliseum—would be a much better education than anything he could possibly get in the fifth grade at Sylvan Park; as for Little Mike, he would just be starting kindergarten the following fall and could go half-fare. Besides, it would give him a chance to get away from the pressures and politics of work, which had worsened steadily over the years, especially since he had been made a partner, until finally last year Don had collapsed bleeding on the toilet. It was a serious bout of Crohn's disease, which kept him hospitalized for two and a half weeks. Though the doctors didn't know very much about Crohn's, it was most common in bright young professionals and intellectuals in their twenties and early thirties, and they suspected it had something to do with stress. Don took it as a warning, and decided that a vacation with the family would be just the ticket.

And so they went, boarding one of the first 747 jumbo jets to cross the U.S., and they would stop to say hello to Rose who came to greet them at Kennedy Airport, and take off again to cross the Atlantic. On the way to the airport on the San Diego Freeway, Little Mike saw an oil rig that was shaped like the Eiffel Tower. "Are we in Paris yet?" he said.

Europe: What a town!

When they returned from their grand tour, something happened to Don; it was as if he started waking up. He wasn't sure what it was, exactly, but suddenly he didn't understand what he was *doing* anymore. Anyhow, in Europe he grew a beard; when he came back to work it was clear the partners didn't like it one single bit.

There was a chill in the air, and it smelled like winter in the wind. Fanny had noticed this the first year they moved to California. It smelled vaguely smoky, almost like burning leaves, which was impossible because no one burned leaves here; there were no leaves to burn, for mostly they remained on the trees—anyway, the smell was intoxicating, and moved people to light logs in their fireplaces and make stew. Everyone was still talking about the Sharon Tate murder, and now Fanny was fanatical about locking the doors. She thought about the time when Little Mike was two and a half years old and he walked all the way to the grocery store wearing just a diaper without her even noticing he was gone. The phone had rung, and it was the manager of the store. "Hello, Mrs. Kelbow," he said in an oddly cheerful tone. "I'm here with your son Little Mike."

"That's impossible," said Fanny. "He's here with me. He's just in the next room."

"That's funny," said the manager. "Because he's standing right next to me!" Fanny dropped the phone and went and looked in the den, where she thought Little Mike was playing with his toys; she was astonished to find he wasn't anywhere in the house.

"I'll be right over," said Fanny into the receiver, and she drove the Chevy like a madwoman five blocks to the market, and there indeed was Little Mike, sitting up on the counter in the liquor department, entertaining the manager. "What happened?" breathed Fanny as she snatched up her baby.

"I found him trying to break into the bubble-gum machine," said the manager.

Fanny never let him out of her sight again.

Tired of his goody-goody image at school, Andrew finally accepted his friend Enrique's invitation one lunchtime to cut school and go watch *Bewitched* at his house. Although he wasn't missing any class time, the kids weren't allowed to leave the school yard at all during the day, so this departure was significant, and in fact it scared the shit out of Andrew even though Enrique's house was only half a block away, and they'd be able to get back in plenty of time before the 1:00 bell. Enrique's house was dark and eerie. He lived alone with his father, who always seemed to be asleep in his bedroom, or else he wasn't home. His brother and sister were much older; in fact his brother had already graduated from high school, and they were never home either. Enrique had a big Jimi Hendrix poster in his bedroom that said "Are You Experienced?" and Andrew realized right away that this made Enrique much cooler than Andrew could ever hope to be.

Tennis Kelbow

It was Fanny's belief that Andrew would excel at anything he attempted. To be on the safe side, she wouldn't allow him to try anything at which he was not likely to succeed. Underneath this thinking was Fanny's deep conviction that if Andrew really *wanted* to succeed at something, he would; nothing could possibly stop him.

Andrew got it in his head that he wanted to learn to play tennis.

Andrew may not have been the most athletic boy in Van Nuys, but at the age of nine he was beginning to grow out of his baby fat, and Fanny and Don agreed that any well-rounded young man in Southern California ought to know how to wield a racquet.

Fanny discussed the tennis idea with Lucinda, a neighborhood woman whose son, Jason, was the same age as Andrew. Lucinda happened to know a tennis pro who was offering lessons in Balboa Park on Thursday afternoons. The two women signed up their boys, who often played together after school, and the kids practiced their strokes with handsome Mark the tennis pro while the two women lay on a blanket on the grass next to the courts and Little Mike swung like a monkey on the jungle gym. As the women watched their boys, they revealed personal things to each other, things concerning their sex lives with their husbands—things they would never have considered sharing with even their closest friends. The fact that they were merely neighbors bestowed upon their relationship the recklessness of almost-anonymity.

By the sixth week of lessons, Lucinda had confided to Fanny that her husband was having an affair. She had no absolute proof; she just knew it in her gut. Fanny was horrified. She was more horrified than the situation justified, considering that she barely knew this woman and had never even met her husband. She was horrified. "Just ignore it," was Fanny's advice to Lucinda, "and maybe he'll stop."

Lucinda thought about it. "Or I could murder him," she said, "and kill that adulterous bitch he's screwing."

The two were quiet. They watched as Andrew popped a ball over the high Cyclone fence of the court for the fourth time in ten minutes.

"If things get really bad," said Fanny, "you should leave him before he gets a chance to leave you."

By the eighth week, Jason was making rapid progress in the areas of backhands and serves and Andrew was not. In fact, handsome Mark the tennis pro was rather impressed with Jason; Jason was one of the most talented kids he had seen.

That was the end of tennis lessons for Andrew: such was Fanny's decree.

～～

Fanny began to feel funny about her intimacy with Lucinda, almost as if knowing someone whose marriage was in trouble might put a jinx on her own.

Even though her marriage with Don was perfect in every way.

Eventually Fanny and Lucinda stopped seeing each other altogether, except for the occasional wave from the driveway, which Fanny found vaguely embarrassing. A few years later, after Lucinda and Tom had moved away, Fanny heard through the grapevine that Tom did indeed leave her and Lucinda ended up marrying handsome Mark the tennis pro, who was eight years her junior.

Andrew never picked up a tennis racquet again.

The Unthinkable

Fanny's marriage ended four months later in a cherry tree at U-Pick-Em Orchard in Beaumont, California. In the Mojave. Fanny had her tin bucket on the ground, and she was at the top of the ladder with half her body in the tree. She sang:

> *Moha-vay. Oh, oh.*
> *Cantah-ray. Oh oh oh oh.*

She picked the cherries and threw them one by one into the bucket on the ground so they made a rhythmic hollow metallic sound falling down. Sometimes one bounced out. Sometimes she ate one. Her children were in another tree, in another part of the orchard. Don came over and said, "Well, Fanny. I've had about enough. I'll drop you and the kids off at home, then I'm leaving with the Chevy and I'm not coming back."

Fanny said, "That's what you think, buster. You may be leaving, but you're not taking any Chevy." It was a white Impala convertible, 1961, with a red interior. Don's Buick was in the shop, as usual.

Don said, "You can have the kids and the house and the Lincoln, Fanny. I'm not asking for anything but the Chevy."

Fanny said, "No deal."

And so it happened that when Don left Fanny he had to call a taxicab from the house in Van Nuys and wait forty-five minutes for the cab to pick him up, which was just too bad because Fanny and Don had bought that car with Fanny's money when they got married, money that she had inherited from her father, and since God knows there wasn't much of it, she wasn't about to let Don drive it over the hill and vanish with it forever. So Don sat there waiting for the cab, sitting next to a suitcase he had already packed, and Andrew and Little Mike sat on the orange vinyl couch of their childhood and stared at him. Finally Don said, "Don't worry, guys. We'll see each other all the time. Every Sunday."

Little Mike said, "I'm not worried, Dad," and that was the last thing Little Mike said for six months.

The Quiet Time

They came to call Little Mike's mute period "The Quiet Time." In Fanny's house at dinnertime, over cabbage soup, Andrew said, "I don't know. It's kind of nice with him not yakking away all the time."

Little Mike wouldn't eat his cabbage soup. This was not out of protest or obstinacy, it was just that he didn't like it; he preferred steak.

Fanny said, "If your father hadn't abandoned us in order to run off with that secretary of his, we'd be having something a little more substantial than cabbage soup."

Andrew said, "Mom . . ."

Fanny knew that what she was doing was wrong, but she couldn't stop herself.

"That man," she said. "That man is the most selfish son of a bitch I have ever met. He doesn't give a damn what happens to any of us."

Little Mike looked down at his soup, not even playing with the translucent shreds of cabbage that floated in the oily broth. This is what he was thinking:

Tinkertoy and Etch-A-Sketch
Lincoln Logs and Tonka truck
G.I. Joe and Barbie doll
Mickey Mouse and Batmobile

These were the things that were important to him, and he had all of them, except Barbie doll and Batmobile.

When Little Mike was a baby he was the cutest thing. As a toddler he used to sit in the bathtub with a white peak of baby shampoo on his head, and wash the tile walls with his washcloth, "playing Pilar." But he drank too much milk, didn't get the necessary nutrients. When at last he became anemic, he outgrew milk and cultivated a passion for meat. In fact he started eating too much meat. He never liked vegetables, except cucumbers because they tasted like the sky. But he wouldn't eat string beans or broccoli; cauliflower was out of the question. To get his way, he would turn blue. Fanny and Don would stand over him, terrified, watching as he writhed around on the carpet in his blue, babylike fashion, Fanny screaming at Don to do something, Don not wanting to give in to Little Mike on the terms of his tantrum, but then finally relenting rather than risk his son's death by asphyxiation. Afterward Don would berate himself. He would say, "He's not going to kill himself, Fan. All human beings have something called a survival instinct."

"No," said Fanny. "Not Little Mike. He'd rather die than give up a fight."

Now Little Mike was five years old, too old for tantrums. This was a fortunate thing, because if Little Mike held his breath waiting for Don to come back home, the boy would perish.

Andrew, for his part, missed his father's solid presence, his height. He missed walking around the corner to sit on the curb waiting for Don to get home from work when it stayed light very late in the summer, dropping sticks and spiky seed pods down the long black gaping rectangle that led to the sewer. When he came, after an eternity, Don would fling open the car door and Andrew would climb onto his lap, place his hands firmly on the huge circle of the steering wheel, and "drive" home. But Andrew liked Don best when he was stretched out on the carpet in the den in front of the TV, wearing the soft maroon wool sweater with suede elbow patches that he had worn since college; Don spanned the entire length of the sofa. Andrew would rub his dad's bristly cheeks and count the lines of crinkly crow's-feet touching the outer corners of his eyes.

Now Fanny and Andrew sat in front of the TV with bowls of jamoca almond fudge ice cream in their laps and watched the final episode of *Laugh-In*. Little Mike went to the closet and pulled out a TV tray, which he unfolded and set in front of him on its rickety legs. On it he placed a bowl of vanilla ice cream: vanilla was the only flavor he liked other than daiquiri ice, and Fanny wouldn't let him have both together because the idea of it made her want to throw up. The boys fell asleep after a while, curled up on the couch, and when *Laugh-In* was over ("Say 'good night,' Dick." "Good night, Dick."), Fanny picked up Little Mike in her arms and carried him to the boys' room, where she deposited him in the bottom bunk, next to his bear. Andrew followed, round-faced, sleepy; he climbed the ladder and fell into bed.

Fanny kissed them and turned off the light, and then she sat smoking cigarettes and playing solitaire on the carpet in front of the TV, the volume turned low. It was a big color TV, the one that Don had bought on Andrew's birthday three years ago, before any of their friends had color. It was a Magnavox console: a magnificent consolation prize. She would probably be up most of the night watching old movies—first *The Late Show*, then *The Million Dollar Movie*, and then, if neither of those was satisfying enough, *The Late Late Show*. These days it was no use even trying to fall asleep. Her bed was too big.

Little Mike, in the dark, could hear his brother breathing regularly, like sleep. But the eyes of both boys were wide open against the night.

"Mike?" said Andrew, very softly.

Little Mike stared into the black beams of the upper bunk, waiting.

"Mikey," he said, "I don't think Dad is a monster."

Little Mike tried to think of his father and, oddly, couldn't conjure up a picture in his mind. He saw him only from the neck down, dressed in a gray suit, holding a briefcase, or a suitcase. He was getting into the backseat of a strange old car, right in their driveway. When he saw his father's head, finally, it was the giant head of a *Tyrannosaurus rex*.

"Do you think he is?" said Andrew.

Little Mike hugged his bear, and neither of them slept.

Little Mike's bear's name was Steak. He took Steak everywhere with him. In the days before The Quiet Time, Little Mike always said that Steak's favorite food was steak. That boy loved red meat.

Sure as his promise, Don picked up the kids every Sunday. He pulled his new Mercedes into the driveway, under the shade of the big walnut tree, and beeped the horn. He didn't want to go in. Fanny got to keep the Chevy in the end, and Don bought a new Mercedes to cheer himself up. This made Fanny so mad that she couldn't even look at the man anymore without exploding. Yet sometimes she found herself wishing that he would come in the house and say hello at least, and maybe stay for dinner with the kids. But when she came to her senses again, she hated him, and she resolved never to remarry, even if it meant she'd be doomed to a life of insomnia.

Don took the boys to his apartment in Santa Monica. It was right on the beach near Synanon, in a run-down, rangy old building from Santa Monica's glory days, the 1920s. It was called the Sandcastle. In fifteen years this building would be spiffed up, painted sea-foam green, and turned into expensive condominiums. But now its old white paint had turned grayish and was peeling off in curly sheets and inside it was a little creepy in the stairwells; in other words, it still had charm.

Don had a small one-bedroom on the seventh floor, overlooking the beach. He stayed upstairs in the apartment and threw the *I Ching* all afternoon. At the beach Little Mike had two corn dogs. Andrew had a corn dog and a cheese-on-a-stick and they both had lemonade with a lot of extra sugar. They went swimming in the ocean right after they ate and they didn't get cramps. Then they walked over to the Royal Motor Inn and rode the elevator up to the fifteenth floor, their beach towels dragging behind them. When they came back down and walked through the lobby to the pool in back, their plan had worked: the hotel management thought they were legitimate guests who had just come down from their room. They went swimming in the pool at the Royal Motor Inn so they wouldn't have to take a shower when they got back to Don's. They left their sand at the bottom of the pool; they could see the grains that had sifted down to the steps where they were now sitting.

A fat old man swam over to them. He was wearing glasses even though he was in the pool. He looked at Little Mike. "Hey, partner," he said. He was the grandfather type. Little Mike and Andrew stared at him. "Hey, guy," said the old man.

Andrew said, "He's deaf, he can't hear you. He's also mute." The man said that he was sorry. "He swims like a fish," said Andrew. "A deaf, mute fish." Little Mike shot out underwater, to the deep end of the long pool. He never wanted to come up. He turned around at the far end and didn't resurface until he completed a lap. "My brother can hold his breath a long time," said Andrew. "He has enormous lungs."

They stayed in the pool until it was almost dark, Little Mike exploring the depths, sprawling underwater like a phantom. When Andrew finally lured him out, his lips looked black against his white skin. Andrew wrapped the big towel around his little brother's thin shoulders. He kissed the top of his small wet head. "My little fish," he said, and they walked across Pico Boulevard like that, shivering.

When they got back to their father's apartment, there was a Ravi Shankar raga playing on the turntable. Don was on the phone, whispering almost, his eyes squinting, laughing. The room smelled of sandalwood. There was a stick of incense burning on the table and the ash had fallen like a worm into the ash-tray that said "Dodger Blue." The smoke rose straight up in a thin stream. Little Mike put his finger into the worm and tasted the ash, thinking that his father's life was pathetic.

"I thought we'd get some pizza for dinner," said Don when he got off the phone. "How does that sound?"

"No," said Andrew. "Little Mike wants steak."

The Tacos of My Heart

Miguelito was watching television. His little face was so close to the big box; he was huddled in a blanket in the brown armchair. Pilar washed the scouring powder down the sides of the kitchen sink, rinsing until the porcelain was slick. Mrs. Kelbow had gone to Beverly Hills; she wouldn't be back until four. Pilar dried her hands on a dish towel and went in to see her baby. "Miguelito," she said, "you will hurt your eyes. You should not sit so close."

Miguelito went on staring at the screen, which didn't have lines of white light and black, like the TV at the home of Pilar and Ken, and it didn't turn into a little white-hot pinpoint of light that stayed on the screen long after you turned it off. Instead it showed gaudy flashes of colored light, red and green and blue, and even if you turned the sound all the way down, there was a terrible high-frequency noise that always came out of the box—out of the box and into Miguelito's ears, and who knew what that noise was? It was a bad TV. Pilar pushed the heavy armchair back a few feet, so Miguelito was a little farther away from the television. "*Corazón mio*," she said. "What can I make you for your lunch?"

Pilar knew that Miguelito wasn't talking, but anyway she talked to him. "You want a taco?" she said, and Miguelito looked up at her, what a sweet little boy he was, and nodded as if to say, yes, Pilar, *cuidaniños de mi sueños*, I would love to have for lunch one of your most delicious tacos, I only wish you had time to make some delicious homemade tortillas for me and that you didn't have to wax the floor. And I wish also that your back didn't hurt and that you didn't feel dizzy when you cleaned the oven with Easy-Off oven cleaner, which burns your fingers right through the rubber gloves, and I wish you didn't have to clean the toilets every time, but go ahead and relax, *un momentito*, and make me lunch because Mrs. Kelbow won't be back until four o'clock today.

"Miguelito," said Pilar, "*el placer es el mío*."

The First Big One

As the sun rose on February 9, 1971, a hot wind blew through Los Angeles, the Santa Ana wind, blowing smog across the periwinkle sky over the San Fernando Valley, buffeting the brown air up against the foothills of the Santa Monica Mountains. Dogs barked all over the valley, and somewhere in the foothills a coyote howled.

At 6:06 in the morning the ground started shifting along a fissure called the San Andreas Fault. A solid crystal bird she had bought in Murano, Italy, fell off the bookshelf in Fanny Kelbow's living room and bounced on the pegged and grooved hardwood floor. The earth started moving, gathering force, rumbling. The water sloshed in the pool. Peanuts woke up and barked. Glass broke everywhere. It's true that televisions didn't career through the air, knocking their owners unconscious as they would when the earth would shake again twenty-three years later; nevertheless, when Fanny awakened she thought of nuclear holocaust. She jumped out of bed and fell against the dresser. A crack appeared in Van Norman Dam, causing scary seepage. A freeway overpass broke in half in Palmdale; four commuters couldn't brake fast enough and drove downward toward death. Fanny made her way through the house, shouting for her boys, bumping into furniture. There was a horrible thundering noise and the shattering sound of a thousand chandeliers falling in the street. The sliding glass door of the living room opened and the swimming pool poured onto the wood floor. A hospital collapsed in Sylmar. All Fanny could think of was the bunk beds.

Sixty seconds or sixty years later, Fanny reached the boys' room. Andrew was standing in the doorway, bracing himself against the frame. The earth slowed down and stopped; the earthquake noise, the rumbling, the sound of breaking glass gradually subsided. Fanny hugged Andrew to her breast, nearly crushing him. She pulled him over to the bed, where Little Mike still lay. Little Mike was grinning.

Little Mike spoke.

"Wow," he said. "I loved that."

After that, all the people who lived in Los Angeles were acutely aware of what was over their heads at any given moment. The next day, Fanny pulled the swag lamp down out of the boys' room; she removed the bookshelves from up above her own headboard.

"Now listen, kids," she said, putting them to bed one night, "if, God forbid, that ever happens again, I want you to put your pillow over your head."

"Like this?" said Andrew. He wore it like a huge hat, standing on his knees on Little Mike's bed.

"And if it ever happens when you're at school, then come

straight home. And don't forget to pick up Little Mike at the kindergarten."

"The biggest earthquake ever was in Japan in 1923, and it was a nine point seven on the Richter scale," said Andrew.

"Big deal," said Little Mike. "You think you're so smart."

"I *am* so smart."

"Are not."

"Am so."

Et cetera.

"I bet you can't spell 'antidisestablishmentarianism,'" said Andrew.

"Why would I want to?" said Little Mike. "I'm the greatest."

"No, I'm the greatest," said Andrew.

"No, I'm the greatest." Et cetera.

At school, asphalt had buckled, buildings were condemned. Classes had to be moved into the bungalows out in the school yard; they were too small, they were hot, they were poorly ventilated. Teachers complained.

An earthquake-preparedness demonstration was held in the auditorium—Fanny was there. "Let's be prepared, for a change," she said when she got home, and she concocted a plan to assemble an earthquake-survival kit. She ordered four five-gallon glass bottles of Sparkletts water to keep in the garage at all times, and she kept lots of canned food in the pantry. But somehow she never got around to candles, flashlights, batteries, aspirin, bandages, a manual can opener, thick-soled sneakers for walking through the streets full of broken glass; nor did she ever learn how to turn off the gas, although she, and just about everyone else in Southern California, kept meaning to.

Fanny Fell
(and It Was Swell)

Fanny went back to work. The paltry check Don handed her most months couldn't feed her children as well as they deserved. Fanny also knew it would do her good to get out of the house every day: she felt pickled in her bathrobe. Therefore she went to work for a movie company in Beverly Hills in the old Fox Wilshire Building. Maybe the building was decrepit, and maybe the company only made B pictures, and maybe she did get the job because one of the principals was a client of Don's, but one day Fanny saw Elvis in the elevator. Elvis!!

Fanny said, "Elvis? Is it really you?" though as soon as she said it she knew how stupid it sounded, and of course it was obvious, from his sideburns and white jumpsuit, that it was indeed the King.

Elvis looked down at Fanny and said, "Yeah, babe. I'm all here."

"Aren't you hot?" said Fanny. It was summer and Elvis's jumpsuit was leather.

It turns out Elvis was going to see his dentist in the building, the notorious "Dr. Feelgood" who killed Elvis in the end by giving him all those prescription drugs that he didn't actually (medically) need. But that was years later.

Meanwhile, Fanny took all this, this seeing Elvis in the elevator all duded up in white, as an omen, though of what, she didn't know.

And it just so happened that Fanny fell in love that very day. She fell in love on the penthouse rooftop of the Fox Wilshire, fell in love amid the dried-out succulents and scraggly weeds of the roof garden of Montgomery Productions, fell in love with Montgomery Garabedjian, producer-director. That's right, Fanny fell in love with a hyphenate, her boss. Don's client.

Fanny lost twenty-two pounds and her eyes sparkled in the mischievous way that they did before her children grew: it was a look Andrew and Little Mike didn't recognize and didn't altogether appreciate.

They weren't, however, shocked that their mother shared her bed with Monty in the house right under their very noses. They took it rather as a matter of course.

Besides, Fanny said, "If your father hadn't abandoned us in a cherry orchard . . ." and left it now to her children to fill in the blank with whatever happier fate they might imagine.

Things really weren't so bad for them now. Fanny was generally in a good mood, especially on Wednesdays after Pilar had been to the house. And when Montgomery Productions shot their new feature, *Come Hell or High Water*, a political thriller set in Washington, a production crew came into the Kelbow house with all kinds of equipment and they tacked up an enormous American flag over the fireplace, and the Kelbows' living room was the Oval Office for one long, hot, boring yet at the same time incredibly interesting afternoon.

That afternoon made an indelible impression on Andrew. From that point on, he stopped referring to "movies"; he started calling them "films" or even "pictures," and he started going to see a lot of them. There wasn't much in the neighborhood to see other than major commercial releases; the Sherman Theatre hadn't become a revival house yet. Andrew saw just about everything though, as long as it was rated G or GP and they would let him in. But all the pictures he really wanted to see, *The French Connection*, for instance, and *Patton*, were rated M—for Mature Audiences, children under seventeen not admitted without parent. He hated the M.P.A.A. for excluding him from so many films. "I'm dying to see *The Conversation*," he said one night, and that weekend Monty took him, and told him all about Francis Ford Coppola. Andrew loved everything he saw. The La Reina occasionally had a Truffaut or a Fellini picture, and whenever they did, Andrew would ride his purple Sting-Ray bike up to Ventura Boulevard after school and catch the matinee. His friends, who wouldn't often agree to go with him, considered him a "weirdo" for going by himself, so usually he just kept it quiet.

Fanny was meeting new types of people at work—actors, directors, editors, writers—and as a matter of fact she and Monty were working on a screenplay of their own, one about a white man who marries a black hooker in the Haight district in San Francisco. Sometimes Fanny would come home with Monty, and on those days they'd pull into the driveway in Monty's sleek brown Jaguar XKE and Fanny would leave the Chevy in Beverly Hills; usually then Monty would stay awhile, and Andrew and Little Mike could hear the office typewriter in the study clicking away late at night, and laughter, and sometimes long spaces of silence.

Monty was loose. He didn't try to act like he was their father. He used to be married to a black ex-hooker in San Francisco, in Haight-Ashbury. He had a half-black baby named Xiobban, who lived with her mother up north. Monty didn't sleep at Fanny's every night, just sometimes; he had his house in Laurel Canyon too. Sometimes he would disappear for a couple of weeks, and Fanny wouldn't say a word about him, but still it was obvious that something had sprung inside her. She became unpredictable.

Fanny discovered one day that Peanuts had eaten her bathrobe belt, so she threw away her old white terry-cloth robe and began to wear a red silk kimono that Monty had found for her at a thrift shop in Pasadena.

Fanny's family started eating roast beef and pepper steak again.

It was Andrew's eleventh birthday and Fanny made a big dinner. She invited her best friends, Priscilla and Stan, whom she had inherited in an unspoken custody agreement with Don. Stan had been Don's associate for many years at the firm, but he and Priscilla were fiercely loyal to Fanny, and would always remain so. Don, in the meantime, had quit the firm, started his own practice, sold the Mercedes, and bought a used Volkswagen squareback; all this, as far as Fanny was concerned, was designed to provide him with an excuse for not giving her more money for the kids. Monty was on his way down from San Francisco, due around dinnertime. Fanny made a leg of lamb from Julia Child, coated with mustard paste that turned crispy brown as the leg roasted in the oven, and string beans and new red potatoes (lamb's traditional garnitures), and there was a fire blazing in the fireplace.

Andrew invited a friend from school, Tony Cuevas, whom he had known since first grade. One day back then he had come home from school nervous and excited because he had made a new friend. "What's his name?" Fanny had said, loudly munching raw cranberries, which she ate straight from the colander, shining wet, her favorite fall snack. Andrew's reply sounded like "Tony Quavis": his pronunciation of Spanish surnames had not yet been perfected, and to complicate matters further, these names were invariably anglicized by the teachers at school for their own convenience and the Chicano students' instant assimilation. (His real name was Antonio.) "That's wonderful," said Fanny. "Bring him over to play sometime." When Don came home after work and they all sat down to dinner, Fanny said, "Sweetheart, Andrew made a new friend today. A boy named Tony Cravis."

"Quavis," said Andrew.

"Cravis," said Don. "Go like this: Rrrrrr. Crrrravis."

So Fanny and Don always thought the boy's name was Tony Cravis.

Several years later, by the time Andrew had mastered the "R" sound and still persisted in calling him "Tony Quavis," Fanny began to understand.

When Stan and Priscilla arrived at the house, Andrew and Tony and Little Mike were playing in the den with the new Hot Wheels racetrack that Don had given Andrew for his birthday. Little Mike sent a tiny, lime-green Triumph convertible flying out of the slot and the three boys watched, transfixed, as it raced around the flexible orange plastic track; on its final curve it flew off the track and bounced against the sliding glass door. It was nine o'clock and the firewood was almost used up and Monty still had not arrived. Everyone was filling up on onion dip and celery and pretending not to be upset, and Fanny had turned the oven to "low," but still she was afraid the lamb would be over-done. "Lamb cooked in the French manner," she said, reading out of Julia Child, "should be medium rare, pink, and juicy." She looked up and frowned. "Not grayish brown and shriveled." At nine-fifteen Fanny made everyone sit down to eat, Monty or no Monty. Stan carved the lamb, Fanny watching over his shoulder. "It's ruined," she said. "Look at it, it's gray. It'll taste like cardboard."

"We love cardboard," said Andrew.

"It looks delicious," said Priscilla, who secretly liked her lamb well-done anyway.

As soon as they started eating, they heard the Jaguar pull up in the driveway. Peanuts barked. "Shut up," said Stan. "Your dog's a nightmare."

Monty came in with a suitcase in one hand and Xiobban on his hip. Xiobban was two. Her skin was the same shade of soft brown as Monty's beautiful suede jacket. Her cheeks were round and her hair was nappy and soft. Monty lowered her to the floor and she ambled over to Little Mike, who picked her up and put her on his six-year-old lap. He kissed her cheek, which was soft and plump as a pillow.

"I love you," said the baby Xiobban to Little Mike.

"And I, you," he said.

Monty came around to Fanny, who stood and kissed him.

Andrew watched as his mother's eyes glossed over. He looked to see if Tony Cuevas saw, but luckily he was poking at his lamb.

After dinner Monty gave Andrew his birthday present: a Super 8 movie camera. Fanny gave him a tiny Moviola for editing. Andrew went gaga. Stan and Priscilla gave him a genuine black slate clapper, which they had bought at a professional camera supply house in Hollywood, and a box of chalk for marking takes.

"I told his father to give him a movie projector and a screen," Fanny said to the company, "but would he listen? No. It had to be Hot Wheels."

"He's out of his gourd, Fanny," said Stan. "Forget about it."

Andrew started making movies in the backyard, telling Little Mike and Tony Cuevas they'd one day thank him for giving them their big break. Sometimes he wouldn't let Little Mike act unless he agreed to dress up like a girl to play romantic leads opposite the dashing, mustachioed Tony Cuevas. Little Mike protested wildly, but Andrew pointed out that in show business you had to pay your dues.

Little Mike reached into his pocket and pulled out a quarter, handing it to Andrew.

"What's this?" said Andrew.

"My dues," said Little Mike.

"No," said Andrew. "What I mean is if you're going to get anywhere in the movie business, you first have to do a lot of things you don't want to."

"How come you don't have to?" said Little Mike.

"Because I'm the boss," said Andrew. "I'm the director."

"Well, I'm the producer," said Little Mike.

"Doesn't matter," said Andrew. "I'm the executive producer." Little Mike started crying, and Andrew had to promise him he could star in his next picture.

"Three-picture deal," said Little Mike, sobbing.

"Okay, okay," said Andrew. "Three-picture deal."

When Andrew had all the shots he needed, he'd set up the Moviola on the Formica counter in the bathroom, the darkest room in the house, and cut and splice the things together. He was the only boy-director in Van Nuys who could shoot out of sequence.

I love it!" said Fanny after the household premiere of Andrew's first movie, *Hello, Jakarta!*, a period piece set in nineteenth-century Indonesia. "It's so cute and funny."

"It's not supposed to be funny," said the filmmaker to his mom. "It's about the horrors of imperialism."

"The kid's a genius," said Fanny, turning away, and she excused him from doing the dishes for the rest of his life.

Wednesday

That man's car was in the driveway again.

> refrigerator
> unload dishwasher

At least they remembered to leave the door unlocked. Last Wednesday she had to scratch on the rusty screen of Little Mike's window and wake him up to open the door. Pilar came in and Peanuts was right there. If she gave him the bone right away he would not bark his head off and wake up the household. He took the bone like an accomplice and carried it away into the other room.

> make coffee
> oven
> stove

She was hit with the smell of rotting food when she opened the refrigerator. In the vegetable crisper there were some old limes with hard brown patches like the psoriasis Lupe had on her ankle last year. Under them was a cucumber she remembered from last week that had now grown a spot of mold. How would it look next week if she just left it there? She picked it up to throw it away and it fell apart in her hand.

It was wrong for Mr. Kelbow to go away, Pilar thought. A boy needs his father. Mrs. Kelbow needs

> vacuum-cleaner bags
> 409
> Lemon Pledge

As for Andrew, he was old enough to do without, but not Little Mike. Not Miguelito. Miguelito, *mi hijo.* Mr. Kelbow should have waited until Miguelito was old enough to do without his father. A boy should not be made to witness his mother sharing a bed with a man who is not his father. Not Miguelito.

> Do not vacuum until family is awake
> linens
> bathroom

Mrs. Kelbow shuffled in, wearing red silk, like the *putas* in Oaxaca. She stopped in the doorway and rubbed her eyes. Then she came over to Pilar and put her arms around her and hugged her.

I'm the only family she has, thought Pilar. *Pobrecita.*

Fearful Summitry

"Mom, what's a mill house?" said Little Mike. It was 1972: the year Chou En-lai taught Richard Nixon how to use chopsticks. Who knew that this would one day become the subject of an opera?

"A Milhous is evil incarnate," said Fanny. "And if Richard Milhous Nixon is reelected, I'm leaving the country."

"Where will you go?" said Little Mike, and he started crying. "Can we come with you?"

Fanny took her sweet baby in her arms. "*Of course* you can come with," she said. "Do you think I would leave you alone here with the Milhous?"

Nixon and his entourage arrived in China on the seventh day of the Year of the Rat, which, according to all accounts, was auspicious; plus it was Lincoln's birthday. Nixon performed well on the trip, quoting Chairman Mao at banquets and visiting the twenty-two-hundred-year-old Great Wall. (Fanny wasn't buying it for a minute.) "As we look at this wall," he intoned, gazing ponderously upon it, "what is most important is that we have an open world. We don't want walls of any kind between peoples."

Not even between Republicans and Democrats, he must have meant, for he and his cronies had already been engaged for some time in a covert espionage campaign against his Democratic rivals, planting bugs in the walls of headquarters and such. But no one knew this yet, and when five of his burglars were caught bugging the Watergate complex that June, nobody cared that much. Nobody, that is, except Fanny.

Andrew was in eighth grade at Van Nuys Junior High School, which was attended in equal parts by Mexican kids from the barrio, upper-middle-class white kids from Sherman Oaks, and middle-middle-class white kids from Andrew's own neighborhood. Somehow Andrew understood that before Don left, his family was upper middle class, and now that Fanny was divorced they were regular middle class. One part of him hated this fact, and he felt betrayed, but another part was proud, and he liked the fact that Fanny could depend on him to help her shop wisely at the grocery store. One time, before she got her part-time job and met Monty, she started crying right in front of the meat department because she didn't have enough money to buy a rump roast. Andrew put his arm around her, steered her toward the tuna section, and said, "Mom, it's okay. We all have each other!" And cliché as it was, it was all Fanny needed to hear to completely dissolve into tears, which were partially tears of happiness for having such a great kid.

That Sunday, when Don pulled up in the driveway in the VW and beeped the horn, she shouted after Andrew, "Don't forget to ask your father for a check!" Then she sat down at the kitchen table, laid out a hand of solitaire, put her curly head down on the cards, and cried some more.

Back at Van Nuys Junior High School, all the girls were wearing dull metal POW bracelets. Each had the name of one particular prisoner of war or "missing in action" inscribed thereon, and with this POW-MIA each girl had a close personal bond; his return meaning a great deal to her. "Are you for Nixon?" the kids would ask each other in aggressive tones. The only correct response was "yes," though obviously Andrew was not, since every day he sported a blue-and-white "McGovern" button, which all the kids in his gym class would tease him about. "Of course he can only do two pull-ups," said Bart, an all-American-type blond guy with the physique of a well-built seventeen-year-old. "He's a Commie, for McGovern." And the other guys laughed. The truth was, Andrew was still a little pudgy—his baby fat was slow to melt away, though it eventually would—and pulling himself up over that damn bar required all his concentration and effort. Last year, he didn't come close to qualifying as a Presidential Athlete. But really that was okay—those guys were all Republican idiots anyway. And why were they "for" Nixon? As far as Andrew could see, there were two reasons. First, because their parents were Republicans. And second, they were the types who would always stick with a winner, and Nixon, with the advantage of already being president, clearly had an edge over McGovern for this reason. Following this line of thinking, it did occur to him that maybe he was for McGovern because his family was, but then he decided that there was something in his nature that would have made him a Democrat anyway.

This was also the year Don and Fanny filed for divorce.

Fanny didn't particularly want to; being separated was fine with her—well, not *fine* exactly, but she'd rather not have thought about the whole thing at all. Don, however, insisted and even, bless his little heart, found her a lawyer.

One dreadful afternoon, at her lawyer's dingy office in Hollywood (Don's had a fancy office in Beverly Hills), the four of them sat down to hash out the details; the court date was a month away. Though Don had said that Fanny could have the house, as it turned out he had since changed his mind, and now he wanted half of it. None of what followed was pretty, and a month later, after Fanny went to court, she came out with a settlement of exactly half a house and three hundred dollars a month child support per kid, which is what Don had been giving her (usually) anyway.

La Vie en Rose

A few weeks after that creep Nixon won his bid for reelection, Fanny's mother Rose flew in from New Jersey for Thanksgiving and Fanny's birthday, which were only a day or so apart. Thanksgiving was the only thing that could cheer Fanny up after the election. But this year when Rose came and met Monty she was mortified that her only daughter was

> a) living in sin
> b) living in sin with someone who wasn't Jewish
> and
> c) living in sin with an Armenian

"It's a *shonda*!" she exclaimed, which means in Yiddish, "It's a scandal." "It's a *shonda* for the neighbors!"

"We don't even know the neighbors," said Fanny. "What's the difference?"

"It's a *shonda*!" shrieked Rose, and she started weeping.

"Be quiet," said Fanny. "Do you want him to hear you carrying on?"

"Oh, the Armenian understands Yiddish?" said Rose. Fanny was not accustomed to hearing Yiddish when she was growing up; it was a habit brought on by Rose's advancing years, similar in theme to her sudden allergy to shrimp and other nonkosher foodstuffs that she had eaten happily all her life, until her inexplicable guilt caught up with her.

In the scheme of things, Fanny's mother's opinion of her choice of a mate, or anything else for that matter, counted for very little. Rose constantly berated Fanny for letting go of Don. "That lunatic?" said Fanny. "Good riddance to him, I say. Do you realize that he has to toss a bunch of coins and look them up in a Chinese book in order to decide what to have for lunch?"

"It's called throwing the *I Ching*," said Little Mike.

"It's called throwing away his life," said Fanny. "He quit his job at the firm."

Rose pursed her lips. "He was a nice boy," she said. "A good boy."

"A Jewish boy, you mean," said Fanny.

Rose wagged her finger. "The way that boy cleaned the apartment when Andrew was born," she said. "I've never seen anything like it."

"Mom, do you know what he said to me when he left me? Do you have any idea what he said? He said, 'Fanny, you can have Andrew, Little Mike, and Peanuts. I'm taking Crosby, Stills, and Nash.'"

"No, he didn't," said Little Mike. "He said—"

"Don't contradict your mother," snapped Rose. "That man scrubbed the walls!"

Such was the nature of their fights.

Rose had introduced Don to Fanny once upon a time, and the failure of their marriage was Rose's personal failure. Plus, she secretly thought of Fanny as Anna Karenina and Don as Levin, but even if she explained it to Fanny, her daughter wouldn't understand. Don was the nephew of an old friend of Rose's from Minneapolis, Lou Zellman; actually Lou was a friend of her late husband, Max, Fanny's father, who died when Fanny was nine. Don was an orphan and he was raised by Lou and his wife, Bea, in their big house on Minnehaha Parkway, near Lake of the Isles. When Don was in college at the University of Minnesota, he used to slice lox part-time for Lou at the deli, and Don's chopped liver was famous throughout the small Jewish population of the Twin Cities.

When Don was at Harvard Law School some years later, Rose had the idea of introducing him to Fanny, and she invited him out to the house in Bayonne for the weekend. "That's quite an offer," he said, dreading it but feeling familial obligation, especially because the Zellmans felt he was ungrateful to them for having raised him (though he worked long hours in the deli for four years without pay while he was in college; this apparently was not enough).

When he saw Fanny, it was another story.

Don was sitting at the kitchen table drinking tea with Rose, and Fanny came in the kitchen door, out of the rain. She had a white sailor hat pulled down over her head and she was dripping and smiling. Don loved her immediately.

On their first date after that weekend, Don drove down from Cambridge and picked up Fanny at Rose's house. It was the happiest day of Rose's life, though she didn't let on and tried to act bored as she offered him a little glass of sherry, and Fanny didn't let on that she liked Don because she didn't want to give her mother the satisfaction.

Don took Fanny into Manhattan, to dinner and a French movie. Don was funny and cute behind his horn-rimmed glasses, and he seemed comfortable with himself. He knew how to eat a lobster with the appropriate gusto even though he was from the Midwest, and he would soon be a lawyer.

While they were standing on line for the movie, Fanny dropped a cigarette out of the pack and it landed standing straight up on its end. She knew then that they would marry.

"He's a lunatic," said Fanny to Rose fifteen years later. "He doesn't give a damn about his family."

"I didn't send you to Mount Holyoke College so you could shack up with an Armenian!" screamed Rose.

"Why do you always say 'Mount Holyoke College'? Why isn't it ever just 'Mount Holyoke'?" said Fanny.

"You know why," said Rose, who, even though she'd never graduated from high school had put herself through college when she was in her twenties. The idea was that Fanny should be proud of it.

Fanny knew her mother thought it was her fault, the breakup. "I'm happy now, Mom. Doesn't that mean anything to you?"

"Happiness isn't everything," said Rose, turning away. "Happiness isn't worth a nickel."

For the kids, it was the best time imaginable to grow up: moon walks and smog alerts; sonic booms and superflies; dirty tricks and cover-ups. Not to mention hijackings and assassinations. All these had formed the fragile landscape of Little Mike's child-hood. Imagine: before Little Mike was even born, everyone was *already* disillusioned. Bobby Kennedy was assassinated in Los Angeles when he was two, and from there things only continued to get worse. The summer of his eighth year, the family would sit around the TV watching *Watergate,* which Little Mike assumed was a good show because Fanny got so excited watching it. "Impeach him!" she'd cry, and this was what all the kids wanted too—even those at Andrew's school who used to go around chanting "Four more years!"

Impeachment! What an idea! If it happened, it would be the most exciting disaster since the earthquake. In fact, even if it didn't happen, the mere *idea* of it was the most exciting thing to happen since the earthquake.

Little Mike was at the same time the most independent child in the world *and* the most dependent one, psychically stuck on Fanny. And while he knew in his heart that he was bright, maybe even brighter than the overachieving Andrew, he didn't see any point in pushing himself, since nobody but Fanny would recog-nize it anyway, and Andrew could probably do it better. What-ever *it* was.

And then there was his father. He longed to see him some-times, and to do *guy* things with him, like go to a football game, but that didn't seem to happen. Every Sunday Don would pull up in the driveway and beep the horn, and Andrew and Little Mike would get in. Sundays spent with Don were uncommonly boring. Don never planned anything—never, for instance, got tickets to the Lakers or the Rams, even though he was a fan—or even the Dodgers—probably because Andrew wasn't into that. As a result, there was nothing to do, since Don liked "just being here with you guys." Really—he liked to have them there while he puttered around his apartment, and later the house in Venice, doing little chores or slowly penciling in the *New York Times* Sunday crossword. (Fanny, in contrast, would sit down with it at the kitchen table at eight in the morning while she still looked like a zombie and, using a ballpoint pen, fill it in without stopping, in twenty minutes flat.) So Little Mike would usually go out exploring.

It was on Don Sundays that the youngest Kelbow developed his entrepreneurial interests. One scorchingly hot summer after Don moved into the house in Venice (to live with Nina, formerly his secretary, whom Fanny credited with breaking up her marriage), nine-year-old Little Mike bought two watermelons, cut them into fat, juicy slices, and loaded them into a cooler. He wrapped a strap around the cooler, which he fashioned out of one of Don's belts, and slung the whole thing over his shoulder. He walked up and down the beach selling the watermelon slices for two dollars each, and sold out in about twenty minutes. He was rich. He repeated the performance every Sunday for three more weeks, spending the money on candy and beach food, until he finally got sick of all of it.

In high school, Andrew, having passed the gawky adolescent stage, started hanging out with a couple of cool friends and no longer felt like a misfit. Or, to be more accurate, he *was* a misfit in a sense, but he was a *cool* misfit, one of the "intellectual stoners," of which there were only five or six in the school. What qualified him for entrance into this elite group was that he smoked pot—not with a vengeance, as Little Mike would, but in healthy moderation. Pot smoking wasn't unusual in and of itself for kids at Van Nuys High; what was unusual was that very few of the kids at the top of the class partook. The intellectual stoners possessed no abiding interest in participating in the life of the school—no student body president, Andrew—but, rather, they would perform occasional acts of irony, joining the Chemistry Club, enrolling in Advanced Placement European History. They were the kinds of kids who would have taken Latin and actually conversed in it if Van Nuys High School had offered a course. In eleventh grade Andrew scored so well on the PSAT that he was made a National Merit scholar, and to anyone who looked at his record, it would seem he would have his pick of colleges come senior year. If Andrew had had his head screwed on correctly when the time came, he would have made an attempt to go east to school; as it was, it didn't occur to him to leave his Golden State.

The World of Little Mike

At thirteen years old, Little Mike was on the smallish side for his age. Nature had given him a nice build: at least he was broader in the shoulders than his brother, and his stomach was flat, unlike Andrew's, but Little Mike was undeveloped: his arms were thin and his legs gangly. He was shorter than his classmates.

However, this lack of stature didn't matter greatly to Little Mike because he was a handsome devil, with his green eyes and thick black hair and dark eyelashes, and anyway he rarely went to school, since it had never seemed even half as interesting as kindergarten. He had loved going to kindergarten, especially the part where every day after snack, they lay down on their brown and tan mats on the floor and took a nap. One day his teacher, the lovely Mrs. Thomason, brought in a glass jar and filled it with heavy cream from a bottle. She tightened the lid on the jar, gave it a few vigorous shakes to demonstrate, then passed it around the room, asking each of the children to shake it until they got tired and fell down laughing and exhausted on their mats. By this time the cream had turned into a solid mass. The lovely Mrs. Thomason announced it had undergone a magical transformation: it was no longer cream, she asserted, but butter! To prove this, she spread a little on each of fourteen saltines (although they weren't the kind Fanny bought; they had a different color box, and fewer little holes in each cracker) and passed them around. The children nibbled on the corners of the crackers, complained that the butter tasted weird, which the lovely Mrs. Thomason explained was because there was no salt in it, but she had a salt shaker, and she sprinkled a little on top of each cracker, and the children ate of them again, and together they proclaimed that yes, indeed, it was a miracle—the miracle of butter.

School, for Little Mike, was never to achieve this level of interest again.

So Little Mike *went* to school, but after Fanny dropped him off on her way to work he walked through the massive concrete front doors of the Administration Building of Van Nuys Junior High School and marched directly out the side door. Eighth grade was a colossal waste of time, and Little Mike felt certain his teachers missed him about as much as he missed them. Ever since elementary school his teachers had held him up against the example of his brother the golden boy. "Remember Andrew Kelbow?" they would say to each other in the hallways. "What a wonderful student. *This* is his brother." Bewilderment would follow. "*This* little piece of shit?" their eyes seemed to say. The stigma, along with his lousy elementary school record, had followed him to Van Nuys Junior High.

Andrew was in his second year at Stanford, big fucking deal.

Little Mike missed entire days of school two or three times a week, and on the days he did not make use of the Administration Building's convenient side door, he might show up at Metal Shop and Spanish, but invariably he would cut P.E. and English and History. Little Mike dearly loved money, but you couldn't pay him enough to go to Math. During those missed class periods he went around the corner to Joe's house and smoked pot with him. Joe went to school even less often than Little Mike did; he was in ninth grade and would graduate soon. "What's the point?" he would say. Joe always had the best pot: big green sticky buds from Humboldt.

After missing a day or two of school, Little Mike would write a note excusing himself for his absences. His penmanship happened to be exemplary, and since he had never once asked Fanny for a note, the administration thought his handwriting was parental. Actually, Fanny had written him notes on the occasions when Little Mike pretended to be, or actually was, sick enough to stay home and watch TV, but he shredded these and wrote his own for consistency's sake. The administration of Van Nuys Junior High School believed that Little Mike suffered from a rare lung condition, and therefore his frequent absences aroused no particular concern. And as for his mother, she didn't seem to care too much *what* he did. In fact, it wasn't that she didn't care; rather she didn't seem to think her actions and attitudes toward him mattered. Of course there was a larger issue— the fact that Little Mike would never be Andrew. All this made life easier for Little Mike, though now and then he sort of wished Fanny would act like a mom.

~~~

Fanny and Monty had broken up several months before, or rather they had decided to go their separate ways. Their completed screenplay, *Love and Haight*, was in turnaround at Fox, and it looked as if it would never see the light of a soundstage. Monty's own film company's financing had somehow evaporated, and he was left with four flops and no distribution. (Except for *Shopping Maul*, which had appeared briefly on double bills in drive-in theaters across the country, and which later would play on late-night television. Fanny, with the svelte figure that she would soon lose and never again reclaim, appeared in the picture as a saleslady who is attacked by a dangerous department-store mutant.) So Monty packed up and moved to Eureka, California, to start a specialty advertising business. This was an exciting new venture for him: he envisioned a future that included clean Northern California air, oceans of key chains emblazoned with company logos, and mountains of personalized matchbooks. All that remained of him in the house in Van Nuys was the red silk kimono and Super 8 camera, which languished on the top shelf of Andrew's closet.

He wasn't right for Fanny anyway. Or so said Rose, which to Fanny smacked of "I told you so." Fanny found herself missing him now and then—the guy had a real lust for life. The week before they broke up, he took Fanny and the kids to Santa Monica Beach at midnight on a Friday because the grunion were running. They all rolled up their jeans and took off their shoes and ran on the hard wet sand between the pylons underneath the pier, lunging after the slippery, silvery fish, which glistened in the light of a full moon. When they caught one, falling into the sand and into the water, they'd laugh and throw it back into the surf.

But Little Mike, although he liked the easygoing Monty, who often shared a joint with him, thought that because Monty didn't like professional sports it made him, ultimately, "sort of a geek."

So now Fanny was alone again. And although her children had long ago stopped hoping that Don would come back, somewhere deep in her heart, Fanny never really had. This was not something she would admit to herself, let alone to her best friend when Priscilla put the question to her.

"Fanny," she said, "what if he came back? What if he changed?"

"I can't trust him anymore," said Fanny. "He'll never change." She was beginning to wonder whether it was a good idea to trust any man.

Shortly after Monty left, Priscilla left Stan. She came to stay with Fanny and Little Mike until she could establish herself in an apartment on the Westside. "Did I just make the biggest mistake of my life?" she said to herself every day of the week. "Will I regret leaving him for the rest of my days?"

Stan called her every other day. "Come back to me, baby," he would say.

"No, Stan," she said. "This is best."

Priscilla desperately wanted children, but not with a man like Stan.

"You're making a big mistake," he said. "One that you'll regret for the rest of your days."

What if he was right?

"Fanny," said Priscilla. "What if he is?"

"He's not right," said Fanny, even though she thought he probably was. "Although he does adore you."

"I know," said Priscilla. "It makes me sick."

They were sitting in the kitchen, on the high stools at the counter, Monday, after work. "I think we need a drink," said Fanny. "What do you think?"

"Damn straight," said Priscilla.

Fanny got ice, glasses, Jack Daniel's, vermouth, bitters. "Let's have a Manhattan," she said. She used to make these for Don. She poured two generous shots and garnished them each with three maraschino cherries. "Priscilla," she said then, "there's something I've never understood." She lit up a cigarette, took a long, deep drag. "Why did you marry Stan if you didn't like him?" Fanny thought Stan was one of life's truly great men: intelligent, thoughtful, handsome, funny. For a moment she wished he wasn't so much younger than she was.

"I don't know," said Priscilla. She sipped from her Manhattan, and her lipstick left a pink pattern on the edge of the glass. Although she was thirty-three, she had only recently started wearing makeup, and her pale shade of pink looked like something from college. "I was nineteen, only a sophomore, and he was so worldly. And older. And handsome."

Little Mike came in and the screen door flopped shut behind him with a metallic scrape. "Hi, Mom," he said, kissing Fanny, taking a drag off her cigarette. And then to Priscilla: "Hi, Dad," and he kissed her as well. "Looks like it's happy hour." He lit up a joint.

"What are you doing?" said Fanny.

"Smoking a joint," he said. "Want some?" He held up the joint to her.

"You're too young," said Fanny. But she took a hit, squinting her eyes, as Little Mike and Priscilla watched her.

The Tender Trap

Fanny's second (and final) marriage (of that she was certain) started under a makeshift *chuppa* in Canoga Park.

> Make the sound of that "ch" in *chuppa*.
> It should be guttural.
> It should sound like a spoon
> caught in a garbage disposal.

That is what Fanny's new husband, Edward, told Fanny's kids right before the wedding in his parents' backyard. All during the ceremony Little Mike made that noise, and it came out of the side of his smirk-shaped mouth like this:

> chcchchccchcchcch cchch
> ccchchchch cchcchhcch

only more guttural.

Andrew had come down from Palo Alto for the long weekend for his mother's wedding. Who was this man she was marrying? Why was she standing under a *chuppa*, she who always
secretly preferred Christmas to Hanukkah? In a voice only aud-
ible to Little Mike, Andrew said, "Do you, Little Mike, take this
man Edward to be your lawful wedded father?" Then when
Edward stepped on the light bulb (which the Jewish people
wrap in a white linen napkin and call a wineglass because it's easier to crush) Little Mike's *chuppa* sound effect started up again
and soon rose to a terrible frenzied pitch that blossomed into a
low rumbling mouth-explosion indicating a gunshot from an
unseen foe. In slow-mo Little Mike caved his chest inward and
thrust his slim shoulders forward. In an exaggerated gesture
he looked down at his abdomen, where the "bullet" would
have entered his body. He threw the wedding party a perfect
contorted facial expression of horror, then flung himself side-
long into Edward's parents' kidney-shaped swimming pool,
which was really shaped more like a peanut. Andrew privately
applauded Little Mike's demonstration; later he'd tell him it was
brilliant. When Little Mike splashed down, all of the guests
turned around. Fanny said, "Jesus, Mike. On your own mother's
wedding day?" But then she started laughing and couldn't stop.
Priscilla's bemused expression cracked, and Stan's new (gentile)
girlfriend sneered. "Did I make the biggest mistake of my entire
life?" thought Priscilla. Edward's stately parents weren't amused,
nor was Rose, who was in from New Jersey for the wedding.
Edward peered out from under the high arch of his rather expres-
sive left eyebrow and took a good long look at his new son.

Grand Theft, Otto

Fanny's beagle, Peanuts, and her car, the Chevy, died on the same day. It was Saturday. Fanny called the City of Los Angeles Dead Animal Pick-Up and the Auto Club. The city removed Peanuts, but the Auto Club couldn't start the car. Little Mike wanted to drive it off a cliff and collect the insurance, but Fanny said no. A guy from a junkyard gave Fanny fifty dollars and towed the car away, but not before Little Mike pried off all the chrome horses and pieces that said "Impala." Also he removed the ashtray to his bedroom. Little Mike, like Fanny, was a world-class smoker.

Edward was at work. He often went in for a few hours on Saturday; it was quiet on Saturday, the phone didn't ring, he could actually get something done for a change. Edward was a lawyer. He was a recent graduate of Tarzana School of Law; before that he had been an accountant. He finished law school after four years of night classes, and was among the 6 percent of graduates of Tarzana School of Law who passed the California bar examination that year. Just out of school and finally out of the business of accounting, Edward secured a position with a small, up-and-coming immigration law firm downtown, one that didn't advertise on bus benches. The firm had modest offices in the elegant Pacific Mutual Building on Pershing Square, and most of its clients were rich Iranian Jews who had managed to get out of Iran in the frantic revolutionary days of the ouster of Reza Shah Pahlavi, the days when everyone thought *he* was bad. For some reason the Iranians believed that one should impress one's attorney, so Edward was frequently given gifts of beluga caviar, pistachio nuts, saffron, even several Persian rugs, which Edward laid down on the linoleum and wood floors of the house that Don had once bought for Fanny. Fanny and Edward would now have to buy out Don's share, which wouldn't be easy.

Fanny called Edward at the office and told him about the dog and the car, and by the time he came home, early that evening, with a ten-week-old golden retriever puppy, he had also made a deposit on a five-year-old forest green Volvo sedan with eighty-two thousand miles on it. "How many miles do you think are on the puppy?" said Fanny, and they named the dog Otto. The first thing the dog did was to pee on the ecru silk Persian rug in the foyer.

Later Edward took Fanny to look at the car to make sure she liked it. It was being sold by a private party who lived on a barren hill above Encino. "These things run forever," Edward said, kicking tires, slamming doors. "As long as you change the oil regularly. That's your problem," he said, "you never change your oil."

It was true. Fanny never changed her oil.

"I change my oil constantly," said Fanny. "I like this car. It's nice and square and I like the color. Let's take it."

~~

A few weeks later Fanny received a phone call at work. She worked at the Directors' Guild of America, in the Membership Relations Department. She carpooled with Jeanette, a fat woman who worked in Residuals, and Jeanette had driven that day. The phone call was from the police. "Mrs. Alter?" said the officer, for that was Fanny's new married name. "We have your son here in custody at the Van Nuys precinct. We pulled him over because he looked too young to be driving, so we're holding him for truancy and for stealing a car, which is registered in your name."

"Lemme talk to him," said Fanny.

Little Mike came on the line.

"Hi, Ma," he said. "What's happening?"

"Mike," Fanny said, furious, "you go home right this instant. I'll see you at five-thirty."

The officer came back on the line. "We haven't seen a fourteen-year-old before who could drive a stick shift," he said.

"Yes, he is a remarkable child. I told him to go directly home," she said, "so please release him."

When Fanny got home, the Volvo was in the driveway.

"How did my car get back here?" said Fanny, slamming the screen door behind her.

"I drove it home from the police station," said Little Mike, laughing, stoned. "Here's your keys," he said, throwing them on the table. "They gave them to me when they sent me home."

"Are you stoned?" said Fanny. "Go to your room."

Fanny had to meet with officials at Van Nuys Junior High School that week to discuss Little Mike's truancy. They were shocked to learn that Little Mike did not in fact have a rare lung condition and therefore expressed dismay at his poor attendance record. Fanny, however, was not surprised, though she didn't reveal this to the administrators.

"I promise you," she said, "that Little Mike will start coming to school on a regular basis."

When Edward got home that night, he said, "Fanny, you've got to do something about Little Mike. He smokes way too much dope."

"I know," said Fanny, and she changed the subject.

At Priscilla's suggestion Fanny called the Jewish Family Council to ask for some guidance. "I'm calling about my son," she said into the phone. "I'd like to get him some counseling."

"Well, what seems to be the problem?" said the woman at the other end of the line.

"Oh," said Fanny, sighing deeply. "Don't ask."

Priscilla called Little Mike and invited him out to dinner. She picked him up on a Tuesday night and took him to Hamburger Hamlet on Van Nuys Boulevard, his suggestion. "This is the first restaurant I ever ate in," he said, "and I still love it." Although they didn't know it, they sat in the same red leatherette booth in which Fanny, Don, and Andrew had sat in the night after they moved into the house in the valley. Many of the older black waitresses were the same ones who'd worked there all those years ago, when Andrew was three. Andrew, who had never seen a black person before, had stared at the soft round black arm that put his hamburger in front of him. He stroked the arm lovingly. "Mmm-mmm," he said. "Chocolate." Fanny and Don were mortified.

~~

Order the lobster bisque," said Little Mike to Priscilla. "It's fabulous." As they ate their creamy, sherry-flavored soup and the burgers with pickles and Russian dressing, Priscilla asked Little Mike about school. She was doing a study at the Rand Corporation on school systems and was curious to hear Little Mike's assessment of the Los Angeles Unified School District in general and, in particular, of Van Nuys Junior High.

"It's boring and worthless," he said, "and they don't teach us anything. So why should I go?"

"I see your point," said Priscilla.

Across the restaurant there was a young woman sitting alone in one of the booths. She had no arms. She had her bare foot up on the table, a fork grasped between the toes, an impassive expression on her face.

"I wish I could do that," said Little Mike. He lit a cigarette. Fleetingly, Priscilla wondered if she could be arrested for letting a fourteen-year-old smoke. Little Mike saw her concern. "Do you know what the insides of my lungs must look like?" he said.

The waitress took away their plates and brought them huge slabs of chocolate layer cake. "Listen, Mike," said Priscilla. "I want you to know that I care about you very much. If you're ever having problems, or you'd just like to discuss life with an adult who isn't your parent, I'd be more than happy to talk to you. Any time at all."

"Why, thank you, Priscilla," said Little Mike. "I really appreciate that. And listen, if *you've* ever got a problem you'd like to discuss with an adolescent, please don't hesitate to call me."

Seeds

Fanny went to Santa Monica one Wednesday to meet Priscilla for lunch; she left thirty dollars on the dining room table under the pepper grinder, and Pilar left it there while she cleaned, a visual reminder of why she was cleaning someone else's dirt. Pilar's own house was always a mess—clean, but a mess, because after six days of cleaning, she didn't have the energy to pick up after her husband. Ken's clothes were always muddy—even though he was now a landscaper, not just a gardener—and Pilar always did his laundry for him because he was not capable. But if he threw his pants on the floor, the only thing to do was to leave them there or else the cleaning would be without end.

Pilar went into Little Mike's room. There were clothes strewn all over the floor, and records out of their covers. Mrs. Kelbow had told her that the situation was hopeless, that she should just change the bed linens, put the clothes on a chair, and clean the floor. Pilar straightened up a little anyway. Then she stripped the bed, pulling up the faded candy-striped sheets. As she did, some little things went *ping ping ping* on the floor.

What was it? She couldn't find anything. Maybe she'd find it when she vacuumed. She cleaned the junk off his bureau, rearranging everything into neat stacks. (Don't know where it goes? Put it in a stack.) In the ashtray she found something: four glossy brown seeds and some marijuana. She knew that's what it was; she smelled it. She put a little fleck of green on her tongue. It was. She knew the boys who smoked this in Oaxaca; she knew the men who grew it. She sat on the edge of the bed and buried her face in the bedsheets.

Heat Wave

Andrew arrived home for the summer, and a few days later Edward and Fanny drove up north for six days of vacation in San Francisco and the Napa Valley. Fanny was upset that they were leaving just when Andrew had come home; she hadn't seen him in three whole months. But she consoled herself that at least she'd have four nights in a luxurious hotel, then two in a charming country inn.

The moment Fanny and Edward walked out of the house and threw their luggage into the trunk of the Volvo, Little Mike held up a joint. "Hey, dude," he said to Andrew, "want to torch up a twister?" and the two brothers sat smoking, laughing, listening to Pink Floyd on the couch in the den. They wailed along with it at the top of their lungs:

> *We don't need no education*
> *We don't need no thought control*
> *No dark sarcasm in the classroom*

Teacher, leave those kids alone.
Hey, teacher!
Leave those kids alone . . .

The lyrics meant something very different to Little Mike, who'd failed three of his classes in eighth grade but who was being allowed to go on to ninth grade anyway, than they did to Andrew, who had just finished his sophomore year at Stanford with a whopping 3.9 average and would be leaving in the fall for Italy, to spend his junior year at Stanford-in-Florence, which to Little Mike sounded more like the climactic scene in a British porno flick than a university campus.

They were experiencing a heat wave.

There was no air-conditioning in the house due to Fanny's long-standing myth that her children would die of pneumonia if they went swimming and then came into an air-conditioned house.

One day it reached a hundred and ten. Andrew and Little Mike opened all the windows and sliding glass doors, but this did little to relieve the windless dry heat.

"We need to get some fans," said Andrew. Just as the family had always used rags, or *schmattas*, rather than sponges, so that Andrew and Little Mike grew up not even knowing about sponges, the boys grew up without the benefit of fans to aid circulation. When Edward moved in he was appalled at the lack of sponges, and so introduced them, but no one had ever gotten around to fans.

So Little Mike and Andrew sat all day in their cotton underwear in the hundred-plus heat and smoked dope. It was what

Little Mike called "making the best of it." In precisely this way, Little Mike made the best of every bad—or marginal or even mundane—situation. Andrew hadn't managed to get his hands on any decent buds up at school lately, so Little Mike's excellent weed was welcome. Besides, it wasn't his job to patrol his little brother's excesses; if anyone's, it was Fanny's.

One hot night Andrew and Little Mike were sitting in the living room, smoking pot and drinking big glasses of chocolate milk. The TV was on and the bong had spilled on the coffee table, leaving a big, stale pool of water on the wood. "What would Edward say if he saw that?" said Andrew, slow, stoned. "I'd better clean it up." They both just sat there. Andrew looked at Little Mike and they both cracked up.

Little Mike said, "Let's just leave it like that and tell Edward to clean it up when they come back."

"That is *so* funny," said Andrew.

They became mesmerized by the TV. There was a fire on the local news. "Whoa," said Andrew. "Look at that." There were houses burning, houses not unlike their own. The flames were wild, children were crying, black smoke was everywhere. "Firefighters are battling to control a fire in Stone Canyon," said the newscaster.

Andrew thought for a moment. "Where's Stone Canyon?" he said.

His little brother looked at him through clouded eyes. "Stone Canyon?" he drawled in a San Fernando Valley accent, then he gestured around the room. "Right here, dude."

Little Mike called in sick every day, and so for as long as Fanny and Edward were gone, he didn't show up at the airless telemarketing room from which he sold office supplies at inflated prices under various pseudonyms.

Here is a partial list of Little Mike's aliases:

> Ron Venal
>
> Rocco Lewis
>
> Throckmorton Gazortenplatt
>
> Joe Strummer
>
> Frank Smegma
>
> Al Davis
>
> Ekim Woblek

The only name the office managers with whom he did business ever questioned was Ekim Woblek. Little Mike didn't let on that it was simply his real name spelled backward; he pronounced it "Vobleck" and told them that he was a Muslim of Polish descent. They never questioned Frank Smegma, except one time when a Mrs. Cleary, the office manager of Farmers' Insurance in Wichita Falls, Texas, asked him how he spelled it, then proceeded to order 24 boxes of Rolling Writers, 144 IBM Selectric typewriter ribbons, 12 boxes of correction tape, 3 cases of Liquid Paper, and a gross of mixed pink and blue Post-it Notes. Her large order earned her a premium bonus of 1 small portable color television.

Andrew used the excuse of keeping his baby brother company to postpone looking for a summer job himself, but he knew he'd have to get off his ass as soon as Fanny and Edward came back.

It was hot, but not too hot for Little Mike to watch TV all day long and swim in the warm pool in the evenings, or for Andrew to sit outside under the rubber tree in a long wet T-shirt and spend hours reading *Mastering the Art of French Cooking*, volumes I and II, which were the only books his mother had in the house that didn't have swastikas on the covers. Andrew's T-shirt would dry every few minutes and he'd have to dip himself in the pool at regular intervals, his eyes still stuck on the cookbook. He'd hold the book up out of the water as he submerged himself to the shoulders, then he'd walk mechanically up the steps out of the pool and return to his chair in the shade of the rubber tree. The pool was too warm to cool him off; it was the wet T-shirt and the very slight dry breeze in the shade that helped somewhat.

Cooking became a sort of religion to Andrew, and volumes I and II were like the Old and New Testaments of his newfound faith. At night, when it was cooler, he'd head for the kitchen and try out new techniques.

By the time Fanny and Edward came home from their vacation, Little Mike had lost his job, and Andrew could produce a perfect béchamel.

Chapter VI: Poultry

Monday: Roast Chicken.
Tuesday: Casserole—Roasted Chicken.
Wednesday: Sautéed Chicken.
Thursday: Coq au Vin.
Friday: Broiled Chicken à la Diable.
Saturday: Chicken Breasts (Suprêmes de Volaille).
Sunday: Goose.

Somebody said, "Aren't you getting kind of sick of chicken?"
Andrew had to skip duck (which should have come between breasts and goose) because he couldn't find it at any of the markets in the area.

He remembered his first taste of duck. For his ninth birthday, his parents had taken the family to the Shanghai Restaurant on Hollywood Boulevard. It seemed to him the most elegant place on earth, with its magnificent facade and imperial archway done all in Chinese reds and rich golds. They had Peking duck, specially ordered twenty-four hours in advance. It came splayed out artfully in neat slices on a large ornate platter: careful pieces of sliced breast in the center, with crispy skins and the gleaming crackling legs and wings arranged around it. The expressionless waiter picked up a Chinese pancake deftly with two spoons held like chopsticks and put it on a plate. He smeared a little of the sweet brown hoisin sauce over it with the back of a spoon, then added two or three morsels of duck and a bit of carved scallion and, with spoons clinking, rolled it into a burrito shape.

Fanny tasted it and said, "Duck is love."

Don laughed and kissed Fanny's oily lips. "Fanny," he said, "I duck you."

Then they started singing old show tunes, substituting the word "duck" wherever the word "love" was used. Andrew's father regarded his family and sang:

> *I didn't ask for DUCK*
> *Then you walked through my door*
> *Didn't mean to fall in DUCK with you*
> *Now I don't know anymore*
> *'Cause it's wonderful*
> *This thing called DUCK*

And when the waiter tried to take the platter of duck away before the family had eaten every last bit of it, Fanny held on to the edge of it and sang to the uncomprehending waiter:

> *You can't take DUCK away*
> *Oh no, not yet*
> *For DUCK came here to stay*
> *The day we met*

Meanwhile Little Mike, who was four and a half, emptied seven, eight, nine packets of sugar into his teacup as his parents sang. Andrew tried to come up with a song but couldn't think of even one. Where did his parents get these songs? He had never heard any of them before, and yet they pulled them out of their heads as if they had always been there, waiting, for just the purpose of being sung at the Shanghai that very evening.

Then, even Little Mike, who was shredding a Chinese pancake onto the red leather of the booth, started singing too:

> One, two, three, I DUCK you
> A, B, C, I care!

And Fanny and Don were thrilled. But it was Andrew's birthday; he was four and a half years Little Mike's senior, and *he* should have come up with something. Don looked into Fanny's eyes and sang:

> Hasta luego, for now
> My Latin DUCK
> My heart is on fuego for you
> And so I'll return
> My Latin DUCK

"My Latin Duck," said Fanny, and even though that was not the name of the song, Don didn't bother to correct her. That's how full of love he was at that moment. By Andrew's birthday the following year, Don had left Fanny and moved in with his secretary.

In any case, none of the markets near Fanny's house had a duck ten years later, which perhaps was just as well; duck was fatty and difficult to prepare. Andrew did manage to find a goose at Gelson's, although when he brought it home Fanny informed him that goose was just as fatty as duck.

The kitchen had heated up terribly from the roasting on Monday and Tuesday and the goose on Sunday, so Andrew purchased a box-shaped fan, which he wedged into the open kitchen window, blowing the hot air outward into the front yard and thereby creating a cross-current in conjunction with the open sliding glass door in the dining room.

The poultry was delicious, and the family got a chance to sample some nice cabernets with the roasts and pinot noirs with the lighter dishes such as coq au vin, and Fanny and Edward quarreled, as they would come to do frequently, about the relative merits of zinfandel. For Eureka! They had discovered wine in the Napa Valley. Everyone was relieved when the week was over; the refrigerator was full of leftovers and the family was tired of fowl.

The following week was a productive one for all. Edward won a very problematic immigration case involving an Italian cinematographer who should have been granted H-1 status. Little Mike secured a new position in another phone room in which he would collect on some 90 percent of his commissions. The year was 1979, and Andrew got a summer job constructing pizzas, pulling dough into big stretchy circles, covering them with elastic grated cheese, and scattering toppings thereon.

Fanny went to work at the Directors' Guild as usual, but her baby boy was home for the summer, and this was enough to make her weep with joy.

Love, Pilar

It was late autumn and not quite light out yet, and when Pilar came walking up the brick path toward the house, the English walnut tree was like a big shadowy black man standing in the front yard. There were sharp yellow leaves everywhere, fallen from the tree, phosphorescent as the ocean in the dark morning. Pilar asked herself: What will become of this family? What will become of me?

Otto jumped on her when she came in, nearly knocking her down, but he didn't bark the way Peanuts used to. Mr. Alter was up already, as usual, sitting at the table with coffee and newspaper. He was wearing a blue bathrobe, and his skinny hairy legs stuck out with fuzzy moccasins at the ends.

"Hi, Pilar," he said. "Down, Otto."

"Good morning, Mr. Alter."

Pilar went to the pantry before she even put down her pocketbook and found a Milkbone for Otto. He accepted it in his teeth and took it into the den to work on it. He was more than four times the size of Peanuts.

Fanny appeared in the doorway like a sleepwalker. Her puffy eyes had black circles underneath, and she rubbed them hard with her fists like a baby.

"Good morning, Mrs. Kelbow," said Pilar, and Edward gave her a sharp look.

"She's not Mrs. Kelbow anymore," he said.

"Oh, Edward, what's the big deal?" said Fanny. "I'm going back to bed."

"I'm sorry, Mrs. Alter," said Pilar. She was noticing how old Mrs. Kelbow looked.

Fanny was noticing how old Pilar looked. She said, "Anyway, you know you're supposed to call me Fanny."

Mrs. Kelbow was wearing a pink-and-white polka-dotted terry-cloth robe. Pilar always noticed the clothing of her ladies and their families because eventually all their old garments would be handed over to her in a shopping bag. Her ladies had always done this, thinking perhaps that Pilar had many poor relations who would otherwise go naked, but the truth was that the husband of her sister Lupe owned three apartment buildings in Monterey Park, and they and their children shopped for clothing at Bullocks and The Broadway in Pasadena—nice department stores. So whenever one of Pilar's ladies gave her a bag of clothing, Pilar might look inside and see if there was something she or Ken might particularly like, but she would always take the rest of the bag and drop it off at Goodwill on her way home. Pilar tried to picture herself in the pink-and-white bathrobe, and the picture was ridiculous.

᷄᷄

Shortly after Mrs. Kelbow and her husband had left for work, Carmen came out of Little Mike's room. How old was Miguelito now, sixteen? And his girlfriend was living together with him under the eyes of his own mother and of God? Mrs. Kelbow's household was by far the most unconventional Pilar had seen in all the years she was a cleaning lady. Still, Carmen was a good girl, the same age as Miguelito, and her mother was from Guadalajara, where Pilar had a cousin. Carmen's father was a Jew, a movie director or something like that.

Carmen had already showered and dressed for work—she worked at a health-food store in North Hollywood. Little Mike, who had missed work, would sleep until midday, so Pilar would have to leave his bedroom until last.

"Good morning, Carmen," said Pilar. "*Como está, mi bonita?*"

"Hi, Pilar. How are you doing today?" said the girl. She was very sweet and very beautiful also. It broke Pilar's heart. She had a long neck and olive skin, and curly black hair, which she pulled back from her face.

"Carmen," said Pilar. "How old are you?" Carmen said that she was seventeen. "And how old is Miguelito?" Little Mike was sixteen. He would be seventeen in April. "Did you get your high school graduation?" said Pilar. She asked Carmen this every time she saw her.

"Yes, Pilar," said Carmen. "I graduated in June."

"Good for you, *corazón*. And Miguelito?"

"Little Mike is studying for the equivalency test," she said. Pilar looked disappointed, as always. "He is such a smart boy," she said. "Just as smart as his brother, Andrew. He should go to school."

"I know," said Carmen. "What can I do?"

"How is your mother?" said Pilar.

"My mother is crazy," said Carmen, shaking her head back and forth. "I just thank God I have Fanny."

Little Mike got out of bed at 1:15, wrapped himself in a blanket, and turned on the TV in the living room. He lit up the marijuana cigarette without even eating anything.

"Want a hit?" he said to Pilar as she walked through.

"Miguelito," she said. "You should not smoke that stuff. It will estunt your growth."

"Estunt?" said Little Mike.

Pilar was behind schedule all day because she couldn't start on Little Mike's room until 1:30. It was 3:30 when she was ready to go, but Little Mike's sheets and Mr. Alter's bathrobe still were not dry.

Pilar left a note for Mrs. Kelbow in her careful, loopy script:

> *Mrs. Kelbo:*
> *Please I need for the next week. Vacum cleaner bags and*
> *409 and Ajacks. I left the sheets and the Mr. Alter robe*
> *(blue) in the dry machine.*
>
> > *Love,*
> > *Pilar*

Fanny's Favorite Foods

Fanny would have to say that roast chicken was her absolute favorite, and secretly she thought that her own roast chicken was a little better than Andrew's. Leg of lamb was up there too. Once she saw a sign in front of the Korean butcher shop on Moorpark that said:

RAMB SALE

so she sometimes called it reg of ramb. But that was not nearly so disturbing as the time she saw a sign for a new grocery store on Olympic Boulevard in Korea Town that said:

GLAND OPENING

Fanny also loved ram chops. And lack of ram.

But left to her own devices, as she sometimes was when Edward was away on business and Little Mike was out somewhere with

Carmen, she would make her favorite sandwich, these days, liverwurst on Wonder bread with French's mustard (no lettuce), cut into quarters, and bread 'n' butter pickles next to it on the plate. Here are some other things Fanny loved to eat:

A lettuce, tomato, and mayonnaise sandwich on Wonder bread

A quarter of a head of iceberg lettuce with Thousand Island dressing on it

Corn soup: warm milk with a can of Niblets corn in it

Noodles with cottage cheese ("noods 'n' codg")

Suzy Q's

A bowl of sliced bananas, sour cream, and sugar

She'd curl up on the couch in the den with any one of these treats in her lap and Otto curled up next to her (Edward wouldn't let him on the couch when he was home) and a good Robert Ludlum book, and that, to Fanny, was a perfect evening.

Fanny attributed her high quality of life to the fact that she had said "rabbit" on the first day of every month since she was nine years old and her cousin Leonore told her it was good luck.

Carmen was also extremely superstitious, and Fanny learned many useful things that Carmen had learned from her mother. The first time Carmen came over to the house, she took one look at the dining room table and gasped. The only thing on the table was a vase of flowers from Fanny's garden, and Fanny was a little bit hurt because she had taken great care arranging them so that the table would look nice for Little Mike's new girlfriend. "What is it?" Fanny said when Carmen gasped.

"Nothing," said Carmen.

"Come on," said Fanny. "Out with it."

"Red and white flowers together in the same vase," said Carmen. "I don't mean to be rude, but it's very bad luck."

"I had no idea," said Fanny, and she removed them at once.

Carmen was full of these superstitions, most of which Fanny immediately embraced. After meeting Carmen, if her left palm itched, she always kept it shut until she saw a man in uniform, which could usually be achieved fairly quickly by turning on the TV and flipping the channels until she got a war movie or the news. If she left the house and realized she had forgotten something inside, she didn't leave again until she had sat down, however briefly. She never told a dream before breakfast unless she wanted it to come true. She never put a hat on a bed; never gave a clock as a gift. However, there were a few of Carmen's superstitions that Fanny felt were bogus. She called these "the housekeeping scares," and she said that Carmen's mother must have invented them to make her children keep their rooms tidy. Never leave something sticking out of a drawer, for instance, and always make your bed before noon or there will be a death in the house. Fanny said that if that were true, they'd all be dead, because Little Mike hadn't made his bed since 1972.

Wednesday Night

Andrew used the opportunity between fall and winter quarters to complete his applications to film school—although he had his heart set on U.S.C., he was also applying to U.C.L.A., Columbia, and N.Y.U., just in case he didn't get into U.S.C. "Don't worry," said Fanny. "You'll get in."

"Too bad you're not on the admissions committee," said Andrew.

The coming Friday was Christmas Eve; all Fanny wanted was for Andrew to live in Los Angeles. She had suffered through five years of not having him around much, including the year he spent in Italy. When he arrived at Stanford-in-Florence, he was so awe-struck by Italian life that he completely neglected his classes. Fortunately, he realized this right away and was able to get a partial refund on his tuition. Using Florence as a base, he spent the school year traveling around Italy, even going to Sicily and Sardinia for a few weeks. But that meant that on his return, he still had two more years of school. What torture! Now the end was in sight. It would soon be time for him to come home.

Fanny liked to celebrate Christmas; ever since Don had left, she bought a tree each year, and she and the kids decorated it with cranberries and popcorn, and even some glass ornaments. Edward didn't seem to mind, even if his parents were appalled by it (Fanny never mentioned it to Rose); after all, most Christians who celebrated Christmas didn't go to church. Fanny thought of the holiday as a worldwide birthday party for an interesting historical figure.

It was Wednesday night; Pilar had been there that day. Fanny started cleaning up after her. After sixteen years, Pilar didn't get the house as clean as she used to. Lately, she'd forget to dust the bookshelves, and she no longer vacuumed behind the sofa because it hurt her back to move it. (She hadn't washed windows in years.) Edward pointed out trouble spots from time to time—mildew on the bathroom tiles, dust bunnies in the corners of the pantry—but what was Fanny supposed to do? Sixteen years was a long time. That morning, Fanny left a Christmas card for Pilar with fifty extra dollars in it; when Edward saw it he opened his wallet and added another hundred and fifty. Fanny let out a little squeak of regret when she saw that Pilar had left her a refrigerator full of homemade tamales. How could she fire someone who would go to the trouble of cooking for her? Even if it was Mexican food, which Fanny couldn't stand. She peered more deeply into the fridge to see if there were something she *liked* to eat.

Aliens and Baseball

"All you care about is aliens," said Fanny to Edward one day. He had been working twelve-hour days. They were driving in the new BMW to Dodger Stadium on a Tuesday night. Andrew was home for spring break—his last before graduation—but as usual, he showed no interest whatsoever in the Dodger game. Although he would have preferred to stay in Palo Alto, since he'd be moving away so soon, he had flown down to L.A. because Don was getting married.

"Fanny," said Edward, "that's totally unfair."

Fanny didn't say anything; she just stared straight ahead at the freeway sign:

GOLDEN STATE FREEWAY SOUTH

RIGHT LANES

They were passing Forest Lawn Cemetery and Griffith Park. Little Mike and Carmen were in the backseat, but they didn't say anything either. They were all going to the game—the Dodgers were playing the Mets.

"Fanny," said Edward. "I came home early tonight, didn't I? Do you have any idea how busy I am at work?"

"Aliens and baseball, that's all you care about."

"How can you say that?" he said. Having grown up in Brooklyn, Edward was a lifelong Dodger fan; in fact he moved with his family to Los Angeles in 1958, the same year the Dodgers did. He was wearing a blue satin Brooklyn Dodgers jacket over his T-shirt.

"Okay," said Fanny. "Name one more thing you care about."

Edward thought for a moment. "Football," he said, and chuckled.

Fanny turned around and looked at Little Mike. "If the Dodgers lose, it's your fault," she said, "because you're not wearing your blue T-shirt." Little Mike and Fanny had Dodger caps on, although Little Mike sneered at Fanny's because it was the kind with the little plastic adjustable thing in back, not the regulation kind.

Carmen said, "Sweetheart, will you buy me a Dodger hat?"

"Sure, cutiepie," he said, kissing her cheek. "I'll buy you a real one."

"Do we make you guys sick?" said Carmen.

"No," said Fanny. "You're adorable, and I'd kiss you both if I were in the backseat with you."

Edward wore a black cap that said I.N.S. in big bold white letters.

"Edward, you're going to scare the shit out of all the aliens with that hat," said Little Mike. I.N.S. stood for Immigration and Naturalization Service. *La Migra.* Larry at Immigration had given it to him.

"They'll never see it unless they have binoculars," said Edward. "They all sit in the grandstand."

"Fernando's pitching," said Fanny. "They'll turn out in droves tonight."

"I sat out in the grandstand once with my dad," said Little Mike.

"Oh really?" said Edward. "What happened to his fantastic seats?"

"Yeah," said Fanny. "I thought he had these fantastic seats."

"He does," said Little Mike. "In the first row right behind the plate. But he doesn't get them all the time."

"Does he *ever* get them?" said Fanny.

"Yes, Mom. He gets them about once a home stand." Don had finally started to catch on to the idea that sports tickets were the surest way to Little Mike's heart. Or if not his heart, at least the rest of his body.

"Well, *we* have season tickets," said Edward. "And anyway, right behind home plate isn't very good. You can't see the pitches."

"Well," said Little Mike, "as I was going to say before I was so rudely interrupted . . ." He looked at Edward, who didn't seem to realize this was a joke. His eyes pointed directly ahead at the road. "Just kidding, Edward," he said. "Anyway, Jerry Reuss was pitching—"

"Reuss stinks," said Fanny.

"Well, last year he didn't stink," said Little Mike.

"That's right, Fanny," said Edward. "He had a great season last year. Let Mike finish his story."

"Thank you, Edward. So we really wanted to see Reuss pitch, but my dad didn't get his tickets—"

"I'm beginning to think he never gets those alleged tickets," said Fanny.

"So we said what the fuck, and bought general admission to the grandstand."

"Oy," said Fanny.

"No," said Little Mike. "The view of the field was actually sort of cool: we could shout things to Pedro, and I swear he could hear us. But the really unbelievable thing was: no beer, and no Gulden's mustard."

"What are you talking about?" said Carmen.

"They don't sell beer at all in that section. I asked the vendor why not, and he said it's because the crowd is too rowdy. And you have to have French's mustard on your Spicy Dog."

"I love French's," said Fanny. "But you have to have it on a Dodger Dog, not a Spicy Dog."

"If you ask me," said Little Mike, "it's a clear-cut case of racism. They know that the blacks and Mexicans can only afford general admission, and they don't want them to have any fun at the game."

"Do you blame them?" said Fanny.

"Mom," said Little Mike. "You can be such an asshole. When did you become such a racist anyway?" He put his arm protectively around Carmen, whose mother was born in Guadalajara, Mexico, and drew her to him. "Don't you think Carmen has any feelings?"

"It's okay," said Carmen. "She was just kidding."

"Carmen knows I'm madly in love with her," said Fanny. "We all are."

"Okay," said Little Mike. "Then watch your mouth."

"Mike, please don't use that patronizing tone with your mother," said Edward.

"No?" said Little Mike. "Who should I use it with?"

They rode along in silence for a spell.

"It's just incredible to me," Little Mike blurted out finally, "that all my life you raised me to believe that racism was evil, and then it turns out that you're a secret racist."

"She's not a secret racist," said Edward.

"Let's talk about her like she's not here," said Fanny. "Besides, it could be a lot worse. I could insist that you go out with someone Jewish."

"Carmen's father is Jewish," said Little Mike.

"Doesn't count," said Fanny. "By the way, Carmen, next time you talk to your dad, tell him his Directors' Guild dues aren't paid up."

"Oh," said Carmen, "he's so careless."

"He's a director," said Fanny. "That's all."

"Game time is seven thirty-five," said Edward, looking at his watch. "It's six fifty-seven now. What time do you think we'll be in our seats?"

"Seven-twelve," said Fanny.

"Seven-seventeen," said Little Mike.

"Carmen?" said Edward.

"Seven twenty-two," she said.

"They'll have finished singing the national anthem by then," said Edward. "I say . . . seven-fourteen."

"This is a stupid game, if you think about it," said Little Mike, "because Edward can drive as fast or slow as he wants to make us get there at exactly whatever time he guesses."

"So don't think about it," said Fanny.

———

Their seats were in ideal foul-ball territory—in the front of the second tier between home plate and first base. "These are the best seats," said Edward. "This is where the scouts sit." Little Mike watched through binoculars as Mookie Wilson popped one back in the top of the second. Little Mike lost sight of the ball for a moment, then realized it was heading toward their seats. He stood up and stuck out his bare hand. "No, Mike," shouted Carmen, and she put her head between her knees. Fanny screamed excitedly and ducked. Edward's hand shot out at an angle, but he didn't really try to catch it. The ball bounced off the bald head of a large man right in front of them, and landed in the lap of an attractive blond teenage girl sitting next to Edward. Edward looked at the ball lying in the girl's lap, and the girl didn't even seem to notice it had landed there. Edward looked at Fanny.

"Don't you dare touch it," said Fanny.

The bald man's head had a dent in it, which he was rubbing.

"Okay, everybody," said Edward in the middle of the fifth. "What time do you think the seventh-inning stretch will be?" They all looked up at the official time on the scoreboard and registered their guesses. Fanny guessed first, then changed her guess after everyone else did. "Who's going to win?" said Edward. "What will the final score be?" Then Pedro Guerrero was on deck. "Okay," said Edward. "Pedro's average is .321 coming into this inning. If he gets another hit, what exactly will his average be then? And if he doesn't, what then?"

Pedro got a double, and his average went up .023, just as

Edward predicted. "I knew it would have to change a lot," he said, "because it's so close to the beginning of the season."

Little Mike watched through the binoculars.

"Oh, my God," said Fanny. "Gimme those binocs, I think I see Don."

"You can't possibly," said Little Mike. "He went out to dinner tonight with Andrew and Valentina." Valentina was Don's second wife; they had married the previous year.

"Then how do you explain the fact that he's here at Dodger Stadium with a woman who isn't Valentina?"

"Because he isn't," said Little Mike.

"Then someone who looks exactly like Don is sitting in Don's seat in the first row directly behind home plate with a woman who looks nothing like Don's wife."

"Lemme see," said Little Mike, and he grabbed the binoculars away from Fanny. He looked for a few moments. "It's not him," he said finally.

"You're crazy," said Fanny. "Carmen, take a look. He's wearing a red jacket."

Carmen took the binoculars and Little Mike showed her where to look.

"You guys are missing a hell of a game," said Edward.

"We're watching, we're watching," said Fanny.

Carmen found the place where Little Mike was pointing. "It's definitely not Don," she said. "But I think that woman with him may be Valentina."

"You guys are both crazy," said Fanny.

"Okay, Mom," said Little Mike. "I'll prove it to you. I'll call my dad tomorrow and ask him if he was here."

"He'll deny it," said Fanny. "He's with another woman. That's so typical."

In the bottom of the ninth the game was tied 2–2.

"How many innings do you think it'll go?" said Edward. "I say eleven."

"Fourteen," said Fanny.

"No, ten," said Little Mike.

Edward said, "Carmen, what do you say?"

"I don't know, Edward," she said. "This game is getting dumb." She was much more worried about what would happen if there were an earthquake while they were sitting there. She looked up at the concrete structure that supported the seats over their heads. "This would be the worst possible place to be in an earthquake," Carmen said.

"That's right," said Fanny. "The entire orange section would fall on our heads."

"What are you guys saying?" said Edward, irritated. "Why aren't you paying attention to the game?"

"We're thinking about earthquakes," said Carmen.

"It's not going to happen," said Edward.

"Oh," said Fanny. "I feel much better now."

The Mets beat the Dodgers 3–2 in fourteen innings, so Carmen was right about the score, and Fanny was right about the number of innings.

"I hate it when it goes into extra innings," said Carmen. "It gets so boring." What she loved about the game was the crowd noise, and the acid-clear beauty of Dodger Stadium, and the fact that everyone in the whole ballpark was thinking about the very same thing all at once.

Edward won the contest about what time they'd get home: they pulled into the driveway at 12:12, just three minutes earlier than Edward's guess.

When they got home, Andrew was working on a paper at the kitchen table—he had taken an "incomplete" in a philosophy course and had to write an essay on self-deception in a Freudian case study. "You're not gonna believe this," Fanny told him the minute they walked in, "but Don was at the game. And he was with another woman."

"That's funny," said Andrew. "Because I was with him and Valentina at a sushi bar in Santa Monica."

"Are you sure it was him?" said Fanny.

The next morning Fanny looked up Don's number in her phone book and called him. "Hi, Don," she said. "It's Fanny. Do you have a red jacket?"

The Self-Fulfilling Prophesy

Don Kelbow had married his closest friend, Valentina Gianelli, a short, sprightly woman with masses of red hair, in April of 1982, three months after his psychic told him he would marry a short, sprightly woman with red hair.

Don and Valentina had been friends for several years, during which time Don had been involved in a desperate and tormented relationship with a powerhouse of a girlfriend named Diane. Don finally broke up with Diane after months of fighting and misery, and he and Valentina, who had been his confidante through these difficult months, went out to celebrate. Somehow or other they had a lot to drink, and they wound up in bed together, their unaccustomed arms wrapped around each other all night long. In the morning they decided to get married.

Valentina had two tall skinny redheaded daughters, one nineteen years old and the other seventeen. Both daughters lived with their father, a stern, absent architect who had a house in the Hollywood Hills. The older daughter, Alicia, was a poet; she wore thrift-store circle skirts and pointy pumps, and her thick, spiky orange hair accentuated her pimply skin.

Connie, the seventeen-year-old, was learning to be an auto mechanic.

Don and Valentina got married in April in the backyard of Valentina's mother, Katarina. Valentina's father, a gruff alcoholic, also came, though he and Katarina had been estranged for the last thirty years. Katarina lived in the large Los Feliz house with her maiden sister, Marcella, who always seemed to be in mourning for someone and rarely spoke. Valentina's daughters were there, as well as Little Mike, Carmen, and Andrew, and so was the psychic who predicted the marriage.

Don's brother, Zachary, presided over the ceremony; he was legally empowered to do so by the State of California when in 1972 he became a minister of the Church of Universal Brotherhood. Valentina wore an antique white silk kimono, and Don a white linen suit, and Zachary's second wife (he had divorced La Zanahoria) placed thick garlands of purple orchids around their necks just before Zachary pronounced them husband and wife.

After the wedding pictures were taken, Carmen was talking to the psychic. "It must be pretty amazing for you to meet Valentina," she said, "after predicting that Don would marry a small sprightly woman with red hair."

"Oh no," said the psychic. "I've known Valentina for years. Isn't it marvelous that they found each other?"

It was the first time Don had met Valentina's father, Luco. He sat next to the old man at the long dinner table on the patio after the ceremony, and as everybody feasted on Katarina's *braciolone* and the *pappardelle* Marcella had rolled out and cut by hand for the thirty-three wedding guests, Don and Luco drank Asti Spumante together. Don's eyes sparkled as he told Luco something about himself, and he felt a quiet tenderness toward this old, gruff misunderstood man. When it was time for Luco to leave, Don took his hand and pressed it warmly. "It was wonderful to finally meet you," he said.

His father-in-law looked at him for a moment, then started laughing hoarsely. Don sort of laughed along with him a little, and then he said, "Luco, what's so funny?"

"You're an asshole," said Luco, and he kept laughing all the way out the door.

Fanny Shares a Laugh

"That's the most hilarious thing I've ever heard in my entire life," said Fanny when Carmen told her about it later. "I've gotta meet this Luco."

Stupid New York

Andrew was accepted at every film school he applied to except U.S.C., and he had to decide whether to move to New York and go to Columbia or N.Y.U. or move back to Southern California and go to U.C.L.A. "You don't want to go to stupid New York," said Fanny. "It's cold and expensive and dangerous." He went for a week to check out the two programs and visit a friend from Stanford who was now in law school at Columbia; before he left Palo Alto Fanny called and forbade him to take the subway in New York. The amazing part is that he obeyed—for the first two days. The city intimidated him a bit, suffering as it still did from its 1970s reputation of a place of uncommon danger and violence. Yet he had a nagging suspicion that it might be good for him to move to New York. Its terrific energy uplifted him and put him in the mood to capture on paper everything he saw and heard and smelled.

Fanny called Priscilla, disconsolate. "I'll kill myself if he moves to New York," she said.

Priscilla said, "Maybe it would be good for him."

"Sure," said Fanny. "He'll get mugged."

Eventually Andrew told himself that as much as he enjoyed New York, it would be wiser to be in Los Angeles so he could cultivate movie-business connections while he was in film school—U.C.L.A. it would be. Fanny rejoiced.

Little Mike told Carmen he thought it was good that Andrew didn't get into U.S.C.; it was the first time in Andrew's life he would ever be denied something he really wanted, and this, to Little Mike, was important. He said to Andrew, "U.C.L.A. is a much better place than U.S.C. anyway. You don't want to go to a school where they idolize that sentimental moron Steven Spielberg."

"You have a point," said Andrew. "But still . . ."

"But still, you hate to be rejected," said Little Mike.

"No," said Andrew, "it's not that. It's just that . . . I hate to be rejected."

"It's good for you," said Little Mike. "It makes you strong." He made a muscle. "Like me."

U.C.L.A. gave Andrew a full fellowship; it would later turn out to be a fateful place for him. He would meet Heather there, and later Louellen.

The whole family came up to Palo Alto for Andrew's graduation—Fanny, Edward, Little Mike, and Carmen in one car, and Don and Valentina in another. They all stayed at the same hotel, the Hyatt, which Edward insisted on because they had a fabulous Sunday brunch. Sandra Day O'Connor, who had just been nominated to the Supreme Court that year, gave the commencement address.

Little Mike listened to the long speech with uncharacteristic patience. "What a great job she has," he said. "I wonder how you get that job."

"First you have to finish high school," said Fanny. Little Mike had already dropped out.

Andrew in Love

The day Andrew started film school, he met Heather.

Fanny had hated her, sight unseen, and she never let up after Andrew introduced her, bringing her to Fanny's house for dinner.

"What kind of a name is 'Heather'?" she would say later on. "It sounds like 'Pussywillow' or 'Tundra.'"

"What kind of name is 'Fanny'?" said Andrew. "It sounds like a butt."

Fanny looked like she was going to cry.

"Oh, Mom," said Andrew. "You really piss me off sometimes. Why is it that you get to hurt my feelings whenever you want but if I hurt your feelings you look like you're going to cry?"

"Because I'm the mother," she said.

"I'm in love with Heather," said Andrew. "Can't you please, for my sake, make at least a half-hearted attempt to accept her?"

"You *think* you're in love with her," said Fanny.

"I am," he said.

Fanny looked sullen. "Did you say 'rabbit'?" she said, brightening. It was the first of the month.

"No. I didn't say it; it's stupid."

"You didn't say what?" said Fanny.

"No, Mom. We're going to talk about this. You don't even know Heather, and you're making all these judgments about her."

Fanny was fidgeting. Andrew wanted to grab her and shake her, but he knew that would just make it worse.

"What do you have against her?" he said.

Fanny said nothing.

"Why?"

"Leave me alone," said Fanny.

"Is it that classic Oedipal thing?"

"Yes," said Fanny. "It's that."

"Oh, Mom," he said. "That's so cliché."

"I just really don't think she's good enough for you," said Fanny. "She's not smart enough and she has no sense of humor."

"You mean she's not Jewish."

"That's an understatement," said Fanny.

"You're turning into Grandma," said Andrew.

"I don't care whether she's Jewish," said Fanny. "And leave Grandma out of this. Carmen's not Jewish."

"No, but she's half-Jewish, and she's perfect in every way."

"She is," said Fanny. "I'm crazy about her." She looked out the sliding glass door to the backyard. Carmen was playing with Otto in the pool, throwing his tennis ball and letting him chase it, and not minding when he swam up and clawed her back, leaving long red welts down its length.

"Can you imagine anyone ever being good enough for me?" said Andrew.

Fanny thought about it. "No," she said at last.

After that discussion they both felt much better, Fanny because the moment of discomfort was over, and Andrew because he had gotten Fanny to face a conflict for once in her life. Andrew was so grateful he said he'd make a big Italian dinner that night for everyone. And because he knew Fanny would worry about him for the next thirty days if he didn't, he said "rabbit" out loud.

"It's only guaranteed if you say it first thing in the morning," said Fanny. "But that was better than nothing." And with that the two of them, Fanny and Andrew, left in the Volvo to go to Gelson's to do a major shopping.

Arroz for Fanny

Pilar was so happy because Ken's birthday fell on a Saturday that year. It meant she didn't have to go to work (she used to work on Saturdays, six days a week, but she hadn't needed to for some time), and so she could spend the day shopping for food and cleaning the house, though after cleaning other people's houses all week that was the last thing she wanted to do on her two days off. She preferred instead to work in the garden.

Pilar decided to go to Gelson's. Because even though she knew it would be more expensive than Von's, her Tuesday lady told her they had a large selection of Oriental foods, and she wouldn't have to drive over the hill. She wanted to make Ken a few of his favorite dishes for his birthday, and maybe then he would be happy.

First, in the liquor department, she picked up a large bottle of Johnnie Walker Black Label scotch whiskey. It was aged twelve years. Ken was aged sixty. She bought five bottles, sixty years' worth of aged whiskey for Ken.

From the Mexican food department she selected four cans of

Rosarita refried beans. She noticed that they cost a few cents more than they did at Von's, and for a moment she felt a pang of regret. But this was a special day, she told herself, her husband's birthday, and Gelson's was such a beautiful grocery store. The aisles were long and wide and clean, and the canned goods were stacked so neatly on the shelves. Everything was lined up perfectly, nothing seemed to be missing. It was well stocked and uncrowded, even on Saturday.

From the Japanese food department she bought *misoshiro* (soybean paste), and there were ten different kinds to choose from. She also bought bonito stock mix and nori (dried seaweed), and she thought about later when she would make the miso soup, stirring in the cloudy bean paste and the little white pillows of tofu, and she would use a pair of scissors to cut the black sheets of seaweed into orderly little strips to float on top of the soup. This was the way Ken had shown her how to do it.

As she was rounding the corner to look for tofu in the dairy section, she was startled by a sight. It was two people arguing loudly about rice. It was two familiar people. It was Mrs. Kelbow. And Andrew—she hadn't seen him in a few months. He looked fat. He was saying that they should buy Italian Arborio rice, and Fanny was saying no, Uncle Ben's Converted Rice was good. Pilar lurched forward in excitement, but then it was too strange. She had just seen Mrs. Kelbow last Wednesday, but she couldn't bear to see them out of context. "Uncle Ben's won't work for risotto," Andrew was shouting. Pilar suddenly felt embarrassed being in Gelson's, where she didn't belong. She didn't want them to see her there, especially not Andrew, and especially when she had five bottles of scotch in her basket. She went back into aisle 14 and hid. She felt very nervous, and then she felt sad.

The Evil Chef

During the year Andrew had lived in Florence, he had come to prefer Italian cooking to French. "It's more honest," he explained to Fanny when he came home. "And less pretentious."

Two years later, they were still having the same argument on a regular basis.

"How could you betray Julia Child?" said Fanny. "She taught you everything you know."

"You've got to be more open-minded," said Andrew. He roasted red peppers until they were black, then he flaked off their charred skin, revealing the glossy red flesh underneath. He marinated the peppers in extra-virgin olive oil and balsamic vinegar, and sprinkled capers on top.

"That's so stupid," said Fanny. "Extra virgin. You're either a virgin or you aren't."

"He's not," said Little Mike.

Fanny had her own repertoire of fifteen or twenty specialties, from pepper steak to bouillabaisse to "Rose de la Garza's Texas Chicken," but she always used a recipe.

"How long do you broil them?" said Fanny, referring to the peppers. "I want to remember exactly how you do this."

He said, "You do it by *feel*, Mom. You keep them under the broiler until they're black, just so the skin comes off right."

He made *capelli di angeli* with fresh tomato and basil as a first course, and pork chops sautéed with fresh sage, and string beans with garlic to follow.

"Shouldn't we put butter on the string beans?" said Fanny. "Julia says we should."

"Olive oil is better," said Andrew.

Fanny looked at him doubtfully. When he wasn't looking she put a thin pat of butter on the string beans.

Edward considered carefully the wines they would have with this dinner. Cabernet was Fanny's favorite, but no doubt it would overpower the pork. Yet he felt certain that red wine was the ticket. He had some very nice California zinfandels, but that didn't seem quite right either, too big and round. Something with a softer edge would be better. For the first course he had the perfect chardonnay—a 1978 Kenwood—but the red . . . that was another matter.

Edward really wished he knew something about Italian wines, because he didn't know how to respond when Andrew said that a dolcetto would be just the thing.

Casa de Pilar

For someone who considered herself to be ugly, Pilar cared a lot
about her looks. Especially on Ken's birthday, she wanted to be
very good-looking, or as good-looking as she could be, and that
is why on that Saturday afternoon after she went to Gelson's and
came home and cleaned the house, she went out again—to
Elena's Salon de Beauté on Moorpark Avenue. Elena washed
and cut and set Pilar's thick black hair, and Pilar sat under the
dryer for forty-five minutes until it was ready for Elena to comb
it out and style it and spray it.

"*¡Que bonita!*" cried Elena when it was finished, and she
handed Pilar a mirror and turned her around in the chair so Pilar
could see the back, and even though Pilar could never quite
manage to see the back through the two sets of mirrors, she
agreed.

Pilar had everything ready for dinner by six-thirty, and Ken was
supposed to be home already. He said he'd be home by six. He

had to plant a row of cypresses in Beverly Hills, but surely that wouldn't take too long. Pilar sat down and turned on the news on TV.

The chicken teriyaki was in the oven and Ken was out drinking with the boys. He didn't call Pilar to say he'd be late—he'd just have one more, and then he'd go home.

At seven-thirty she went in the kitchen to put the oven on "low." The batter for the tempura was ready, the oil was hot, and the vegetables prepared, but she wouldn't fry the shrimp and vegetables until Ken was home. She opened one of the bottles of Johnnie Walker Black and poured herself a little bit, and then went back and turned off the flame under the oil.

When the small white pickup truck pulled into the driveway at ten-thirty, Pilar was asleep on the sofa. Ken slammed the car door, and Pilar woke up. She was groggy. What was today and how long had she been sleeping? She went into the kitchen and turned off the oven, then shuffled into the bedroom, took off her clothes, and went to sleep.

La Famiglia

Don and Valentina lived in a house on Anchorage Street in Marina del Ray, the first street in the alphabetical sequence from A to Z, which ended at the marina proper. Their house, a friendly old two-story white clapboard with lace curtains blowing out of its screenless windows, was half a block from the beach.

Don and Valentina lived there with Tommy, their macrobiotic cook, and Lantang Thulipat, an exiled Tibetan lama.

Lantang wore saffron robes every day, even on weekends and holidays; no one ever saw him in dungarees. He was always formal in manner and spoke no English. He was terrified of Valentina. He seemed to Andrew and Little Mike to be a temporary guest, but at the same time he didn't have any particular plans to leave.

"It's a terrible thing," said Don. "He's a holy man and he has no place to go."

"Not to mention the fact that he's a terrific conversational-ist," said Little Mike. The lama smiled sweetly.

"Look at him," said Valentina. "He radiates such holiness."

Neither Little Mike nor Andrew cared much about Don's marriage to Valentina, although they were both pleased to sud-denly inherit a host of Italian relatives. Little Mike began hang-ing around with Connie, who hated her mother, Valentina. They smoked tremendous amounts of marijuana in Connie's car, a classic Mustang in great need of bodywork. The two of them would often sneak off together in the middle of family gatherings and go over to the Bora Bora bar on Washington Boulevard because the bartender would serve them beer without "carding" them. These drinking junkets depressed Carmen, who would stay with everyone at the house and act as if she hadn't even noticed that Little Mike had left.

Don and Andrew made an enormous dinner of linguini and fresh seafood—clams, shrimp, calamari, and mussels in a spicy red sauce, and when Connie and Little Mike reappeared they came directly into the kitchen and filled tumblers with Chianti.

The lama led a silent prayer before the meal. The prayer con-sisted of everyone joining hands around the table for a moment of silence and thanksgiving, and it was a moment that Andrew privately thought was riddled with unearned sentiment.

Being unaccustomed to rich food, all the lama ate was a little pasta, no sauce.

Don and Valentina have a llama living in their house?" said Fanny later to Little Mike and Carmen. "That's disgusting!"

"Not a two-L llama," said Little Mike, "a one-L lama."

Fanny ran through the rhyme under her breath. "Oh, he's a priest!" she said.

"No, he's a beast," said Little Mike, turning to Andrew. "Did you see the way he looked at Valentina during dinner?"

"He's a Tibetan monk-type," explained Andrew. The whole conversation bugged him because obviously Fanny knew that Don didn't have a zoo animal living in his house.

"So what's Valentina really like?" said Fanny. "Is she incredibly stupid?"

"She's nice," said Carmen. "I like her."

"I think she's severely tweaked," said Little Mike, and he went into his room and smoked a joint.

She Turned His Head

The first time Andrew slept with Louellen Berman he told her about his girlfriend, Heather.

"Heather?" said Louellen. "What kind of a stupid name is Heather?"

"I know," said Andrew. "It is a stupid name. On the other hand, I feel like I'm betraying her."

Andrew and Heather had been seeing each other for nine months and they had fallen into a dull routine of sex four nights a week and movies and dinner on Friday and Saturday. Heather was sweet and she loved Andrew, but the thought of getting old and fat with her made Andrew shudder.

Louellen turned Andrew's head when she won the Focus Award, a prestigious national award given by the Datsun Corporation to an outstanding film student every year; part of the prize was a brand-new car. Louellen's script was chosen from thousands submitted by students at every film school in the country, and Louellen was tall and thin and she wore tight straight skirts and had a nasty sense of humor and a silky New Orleans accent.

Andrew wouldn't break up with Heather; he felt badly for her. And he loved her; he couldn't let her down like this.

Heather had no idea that Andrew had become involved with someone else, and to Andrew, this seemed to be indicative of the larger problems that were driving him away from her.

Andrew kept waiting for Louellen to insist that he break up with Heather, or to give him some kind of an ultimatum, but she wouldn't. She wouldn't even ask Andrew to tell Heather he was seeing someone else. Louellen's passive resistance drove Andrew so crazy that after about a month, he suddenly and irrevocably broke up with Heather.

Louellen smiled slyly and kissed her man; then she ran off to a screening.

Magnificent Obsession

After Andrew broke up with Heather, Louellen became obsessed with her. It was strange because Andrew professed to have no feelings at all for Heather anymore, if he ever really had, and he constantly reassured Louellen of this.

"I don't understand," he said. "You didn't seem to care at all about her when I was with her, but now that I'm not, you're suddenly jealous."

"I'm not jealous, sweetheart," she said. "I'm simply inquisitive is all." Louellen frequently drove past Heather's house to see what she could see. At nighttime, if Heather's car was in the driveway, Louellen would cruise up slowly, turning off her headlights as she approached, and then she'd sit in her car across the street and stare at the house, trying to look in the windows.

She masterminded a thorough investigation of Heather's background and current activities; she even went so far as to interview a former boyfriend of Heather's. When she was so bold as to ask him questions about Heather's sexual appetites and prowess, the ex-boyfriend threw a glass of iced tea in Lou-ellen's face. She sat there for a moment in the booth at Ship's, which was the best coffee shop in Westwood because they had a toaster at every table, her face dripping, until the good-hearted boy handed her some napkins from the dispenser.

"Don't apologize," said Louellen. "I suppose that question was out of line."

"I'm sorry I doused you," he said, but Louellen was holding up her hand to stop him.

"Not another word," she said. She looked across the table at Heather's ex-boyfriend. "So how was she, anyway?"

Louellen was one of the most self-confident people Andrew had ever met—it was one of the things that made her so attractive to him. Now suddenly she felt too fat, too tall, her hair was too straight and flat. She was afraid Andrew didn't really love her.

"Oh, Lou. I left Heather for you, didn't I?"

Louellen was lying on her stomach; her face was pressed down into the pillow and she was crying. They had just made love.

"I'm fat," she said, but she said it into the pillow and Andrew couldn't understand.

"I said I'm *fat*!" she shouted.

She didn't have an ounce of fat on her.

Andrew kissed the nape of her neck and ran a finger down the middle of her back.

"Lou-baby," he whispered into her ear. "You have the best body I've ever seen in my entire life. I love your body and I love you."

"You do?" she said.

"Of course I do."

"Liar," she whispered.

Louellen and Andrew spent all of their time together; they ate their meals together and they slept together almost every night. The back seat of Louellen's Datsun was filled with half a closet-ful of clothes; that way she never had to go home to change. But she wouldn't bring all the clothes into Andrew's apartment, only what she was going to wear the next day, because if she did, it would mean that she was moving in with him against his will and she wasn't about to do that without being formally asked to live there.

Andrew cooked for Louellen. He made her elegant dinners on the weekends, and when it was warm they would eat outside on his balcony by candlelight.

But years later, even in moments of great passion, just before they came, for example, Louellen might say to Andrew: "Was Heather half as good as this?"

The Green Thing

Fanny felt safe and happy in the seventh year of her second marriage. When she put a sizzling platter of lamb chops in front of Edward, it was true that he might complain about the absence of mint jelly (an idea that Fanny never could stomach) and it was also true that the thick stainless steel serving platter in its heavy cradle of teakwood was a wedding present from her late aunt Rachel when she married Don, but at least this time around Fanny could be sure that the succulent double-cut prime chop that Edward stabbed with his fork would be just one in a long history of slabs of meat he would poke and chew and digest with or without difficulty in the endless procession of years that could be said to comprise their marriage.

It was only in the green thing, the low heavy sinister sideboard in the dining room, that Edward still felt the spirit of Don. So the remodeling they had done that year had been almost a complete success. (Almost.) Fanny refused to part with the green thing. And it was true that it *was* the perfect base on which to put the big old TV—the new Trinitron would go in the living room; Edward moved the old one into the dining room and put it on top of the green thing.

The green thing had three doors, one of which contained the good china ("the Grandma china"), one of which contained table linens, and one whose contents were unknown because the door on the right side of the green thing had been locked as long as anyone could remember.

No one had the key.

It still bothered Edward that Fanny and Little Mike still called the sideboard the green thing. It wasn't even green anymore. When Edward looked at it there next to his brand-new grandfather clock, he saw Fanny together with Don when they were young and their love was strong. He imagined the two of them together in a Van Nuys Boulevard furniture store in 1963, hair piled high atop Fanny's head, Don dressed smartly for Saturday, picking out this particular green thing from among all the other sideboards and lowboys in the showroom. This green thing must have represented to Fanny and Don the happy long life they felt they would have together. Actually, Fanny could still be in love with Don. After all, she didn't leave him; he left her. Perhaps Fanny's stubborn insistence on keeping the green thing in the house was a last desperate clinging to the hope that Don might one day return. And Fanny would welcome him. Avocado—that's what they called that shade of green in 1963, but to Edward in 1985 it looked like vomit. And the brown paint Edward had slapped over the green wood stain was muddy and only confused the issue. The previous Tuesday, when Edward was home with the flu, he had kicked the green thing. The Grandma dishes rattled.

Fanny's Day

Fanny liked to celebrate Thanksgiving in lieu of her birthday, which her kids were forbidden even to mention. Fanny herself didn't remember the date, except that it was in the fall. Hence Thanksgiving. It was much better than a birthday because one Thanksgiving was exactly like any other—it didn't call to mind the terrible marching on of the years every time it came around.

Little Mike broke protocol and asked Fanny how old she was. "I was born on the Mayflower," she said. "I don't remember the exact date."

"Come on, Mom," he said.

"Fanny, you look great. You should be proud of your age," said Carmen.

"Thank you, Carmen," she said. "Nice try."

Fanny once tried to falsify a legal document. When her driver's license expired, she sent the renewal along with a "correction notice" to the Department of Motor Vehicles. This is what it said:

> *There has been a grave error. I was not born in 1936 as indicated above. No, I was born in 1945, narrowly missing World War II. Please correct your records and send me a new driver's license with the corrected birth date immediately.*

This confused the DMV so badly they sent a Motor Vehicles Agent several weeks later to Fanny's house to investigate. "Mrs. Kelbow," he said, for that was before she married Edward, "you cannot suddenly become younger. The State of California will not allow it." Fanny chased him out of the house, wagging her vacuum-cleaner hose after him, sucking, sucking into the hot afternoon. The agent slipped on a black walnut in the front yard, then picked himself up and fled.

So Fanny took Thanksgiving as her own. It was, perhaps, the single most important thing in the world to her. Last year Andrew had made plans to go to New Orleans with Louellen's family. Fanny liked Louellen because she had distracted Andrew away from that awful Heather, but still she forbade Andrew to miss Thanksgiving at home. They had a terrible fight about it; Andrew had very much wanted to meet the famous Bermans of New Orleans, but he finally concluded that his absence would cause such tremendous despair in his mother's heart that he canceled his trip a week before they were supposed to leave.

He showed up that afternoon at Fanny's aloof, still angry, and Fanny, inevitably, felt guilty. But as she said to Edward later, if

Thanksgiving was the only thing Fanny ever asked of her children, it wasn't so terribly much, was it?

Was it? *Was it?*

It was Fanny's day. Andrew and Little Mike traditionally presented her with gifts on Thanksgiving, and so did her friends if they came. Fanny only invited immediate family and her close friends. Sometimes Rose came from New Jersey, and then she would stay for an entire month, which Fanny actually loved, but Rose wasn't coming this year.

Who were Fanny's friends? Priscilla and Stan. Fanny saw Stan often, along with his statuesque new wife, Melissa, but she didn't invite them to Thanksgiving because she invited Priscilla. Priscilla was Fanny's best friend. Priscilla was the most intelligent person Fanny had ever met. Priscilla worked at the Rand Corporation full-time now, and no longer on educational issues but rather problems of global importance: nuclear terrorism and arms smuggling. She had a Q clearance, and that is why Little Mike was convinced she was a spy.

When Priscilla came over to Fanny's house she could be counted on to correct everyone's grammar. She was a grammar watchdog. And a spy. It had been five years since Priscilla left Stan. His grammar was atrocious and he was not a spy, but Priscilla still feared that leaving him might have been the biggest mistake she ever made or would make. She felt sad and lonely. It would have been nice to have a big snuggly man in her bed on Sunday mornings to read the *New York Times* with her. He could squeeze grapefruits for her and bring the juice in a cut-glass goblet to her in bed while she worked the crossword puzzle or the acrostic in record-breaking time, as a gentle Pacific breeze blew in through her lace curtains. Instead, Priscilla spent a good deal of her time trying to find a mate from within the tiny pool of men who approached her level of intelligence. She prowled the parking structures of university campuses on chilly winter evenings using extension courses as an excuse for hanging around. But the men Priscilla wanted were inordinately uncommon, and when she found someone with potential he was always either an intellectual bully, hopelessly neurotic, or unavailable.

Priscilla came alone to Fanny's house on Thanksgiving, just as she had done every year since she left Stan. Maybe Fanny would have someone there for her. Then they might sneak off together to the guest bathroom and peel off each other's clothing and discuss radical theories of economic history in the shower while the family in the living room shouted and hollered and ate foie gras on melba-ettes. That was how Priscilla was thinking it would be at Fanny's as she drove over the hill from Santa Monica in her new white Saab Turbo.

Thanking God for Something

When Ken said, "What the hell does Thanksgiving mean to you, anyway?" Pilar had to think about it for a few moments.

"I know we're thanking God for something," she said, "but I can't remember what."

"Well, I'll tell you what we're thanking God for," he said slowly. "We're thanking God for food. And for family. And you must stay home with your family on Thanksgiving."

"And you shouldn't talk about God when you do not believe in Him," said Pilar. Ken was a Buddhist. Pilar knew she should stay home with Ken on Thanksgiving, but when Mrs. Kelbow asked her if she would come and help out that evening, she didn't have the heart to say no.

Don!

Since Andrew and Little Mike were required to spend every major holiday with Fanny, *and especially Thanksgiving*, they were allowed to see Don only on the day following. This was Don's punishment for having left Fanny thirteen years earlier.

On Thanksgiving night, Don and Valentina and Tommy the macrobiotic cook had a small bird in the oven, stuffed with hazelnuts, brown rice, and raisins. It was a modest bird, and the three of them cooked the dinner all together, and Tommy, who didn't have a family on the West Coast, was happy to be with Don and Valentina, who were really more like friends than employers.

The next night Don would have his family with him: his brother, Zachary, and his wife and two children, Andrew and Little Mike and their respective beautiful girlfriends (after all was said and done, the Kelbow men really did quite well where women were concerned, didn't they?) and Valentina's two daughters.

All of the children who were coming tomorrow afternoon were in the same situation and had to spend the actual holiday with the primary parent; in other words, the spouse who had walked out was relegated to the number two position every holiday.

Valentina was the only mother Fanny had ever heard of who had been the one to leave her own children.

The Big Ugly Present

Andrew and Louellen had their customary argument on the Hollywood Freeway on the way to Fanny's. The topic this time was whether they should reveal their plans to live together to Fanny's family. Andrew said no, because Thanksgiving was Fanny's holiday and he didn't want to take the wind out of her sails. Louellen said, "Fuck that noise. Thanksgiving happens every year, but a love such as our own comes along only once in a lifetime."

She had a point, but Andrew won because it was his car, a 1980 anthracite-gray Honda Accord. Fighting made both of them tired and sad. It made them feel like babies, like their parents.

Andrew had just finished his course work at U.C.L.A., and now had only to finish his thesis, which was a forty-minute film. He had completed most of the shooting: he had a few pickup shots left, and then he would begin to edit it.

Louellen had managed to raise four hundred thousand dollars

on the strength of her screenplay and the added boost of the Focus Award, and she had already produced and directed her feature-length picture. Now that school was finished and her picture hadn't gotten distribution, she was working as a foley artist, creating sound effects, and always trying to sell the movie. Andrew told her that her real strength was as an editor, and he hoped that she would help him cut his film.

Andrew lived in a nice one-bedroom apartment on Sycamore, the prettiest street in Hollywood, named after the large, well-spaced sycamore trees that lined it. The fact of the sycamore trees was remarkable because most street names in Los Angeles had nothing to do with the appearance or physical character of the streets they represented: Elm Drive had no elms, Orange Grove Avenue was lined with palms, and the trees on Oakwood were short, scrubby bushes, not oaks. On the other hand, there was a statue of Saint Monica at the end of Santa Monica Boulevard in the palisade park above the ocean; La Brea, Spanish for "the tar" and named after the La Brea Tar Pits, was a broad street with lots of car dealerships and ugly billboards and somehow made one think of tar more than other streets do; and indeed Sixth Street lay somewhere between Third and Eighth. Fairfax, too, where all the Jews congregated, struck Andrew as oddly onomatopoeic, though he didn't know exactly why. Perhaps it was the way the old-time locals pronounced it: "Fehr-fechs."

While Louellen's apartment was cluttered and small, Andrew lived in an attractive thirties zig-zag moderne building; his apartment was tidy and comfortable and his kitchen was more than workable. So it was decided that rather than trying to find a new place together, Louellen would move in with him there.

In the car, on the way to the valley for Thanksgiving, Fanny's gift sat on Louellen's lap. It was wrapped in huge bunches of blue and green tissue paper crumpled to look stylishly ugly. Andrew had wrapped it himself. There was a big black ribbon on top of the large square box. Andrew knew that when Little Mike saw it he would say, "It's a record, right?" and laugh raucously. Little Mike had been in a consistently good mood ever since Carmen had moved in, and he had even begun showing outward signs of generosity. He had finally stopped stealing money from Edward's overstuffed wallet. Andrew adored Carmen; he thought she was lovely and exotic and the best possible influence on Little Mike.

When Andrew walked in with Louellen and the big ugly present, Otto jumped on Louellen and nearly knocked her over.

Pilar was there. What was she doing there on Thanksgiving? Fanny said, "Oh, I thought it would be nice if we didn't have to do all the dishes." She looked at Andrew for a reaction—she knew what he'd think.

"Because it's your birthday, I'm not going to say anything," he said.

Fanny looked relieved.

"Except the word 'bourgeois,'" he said.

Little Mike was chain-smoking Chesterfields and trying to look like Nat King Cole. He showed Andrew a three-quarter profile and puffed out his lips a little. "Who am I?" he said to Andrew.

Andrew said, "You're not Nat King Cole." But secretly Andrew did think he looked a little bit like him.

Little Mike pointed to the big square box Louellen was

holding. Andrew said, "Don't say it." So instead Little Mike went to work trying to break into the far right-hand door of the green thing, which had become a shared preoccupation between him and Edward, a funny sort of bond.

Priscilla was cooing to someone on the phone in the kitchen. Pilar was trying to clean up after Fanny, who was deglazing, and Louellen said quietly, "Fanny, where are the dishes? I'll set the table." Fanny said that they were in the green thing.

Louellen knew all about the green thing because she was practically family by this time, but she thought it was pretty stupid to call it the green thing when it was a hideous shade of brown. It was perhaps the ugliest piece of furniture Louellen had ever seen.

The turkey came out of the oven and Edward carved. Pilar was scrubbing the roasting pan already.

"I can't believe you guys missed the foie gras," said Fanny to Louellen.

"I know," said Louellen. "I wanted to leave earlier, but Andrew took forever getting ready." It was a lie.

"It was fabulous," said Fanny. "We should have saved you some, but we didn't."

"That's okay," said Louellen, as Fanny laughed like a demon.

"It's unbelievably fattening anyway," said Fanny. "You shouldn't eat it."

"No, Mom. *You* shouldn't eat it," said Andrew.

"That was mean," said Fanny.

"Well, it was mean not to save us any and then gloat about it."

When Fanny wasn't looking, Carmen brought out from her room four crackers with foie gras, which she had secretly saved for Andrew and Louellen. Andrew stuffed two of them in his mouth at once and when Fanny happened to turn around he started laughing. Cracker crumbs flew out of his mouth.

Priscilla, still on the phone, was getting in Edward's way. As he moved from bird to platter with slices of white meat stuck on the tip of his knife, Priscilla absentmindedly walked in circles around him with the cord until Edward nearly sliced her thin white arm off her body. "Fanny," said Edward, "why does Priscilla insist on talking right here in this tiny space between Pilar and I?"

"In this tiny space between Pilar and *me*," said Priscilla.

Fanny opened a can of Ocean Spray cranberry sauce and slid it onto a white plate. It swam there in a little pond of the pink juice. Fanny sliced it into half-inch rounds with a butter knife, and she knew that Andrew and Little Mike would fight over the end piece that had the impression of the can. Edward looked at it. "Fanny, why?" he said.

Fanny ignored him and went on slicing because the answer was something Edward knew but could not seem to fathom. It started with a T and ended with an N. Tradition. Thanksgiving meant Ocean Spray.

There were times like these when Edward didn't understand his wife. She went to such great trouble to make the fanciest Thanksgiving dinner—free-range turkey, water chestnut and shiitake mushroom cornbread stuffing, wild rice, yam muffins, five other gourmet starches, fresh peas that took her and Pilar three hours to shell, assorted-tuber puree in hand-carved zucchini boats—and still she insisted on Ocean Spray. She was careful to make sure the sauce retained the shape of the can. "Fanny, why?" Edward cried.

Then, suddenly, it came to him: the Ocean Spray ritual was

something Fanny used to perform for Don. "Fanny!" he said, but no one was paying attention.

Little Mike was purloining fat black olives off the relish tray, which sat on the green thing, waiting to go to the table.

"Fanny!" said Edward, now thinking about the green thing. "What's in the right-hand cabinet of the sideboard?" It was the ninety-seventh time he had asked the question.

"The sideboard?" said Fanny, looking around, playing dumb. "Oh, you mean the green thing?"

Edward said, "The sideboard."

"Green thing," said Fanny.

Sideboard. Green thing. Sideboard. Green thing.

"What's in it?" said Edward.

Fanny said, "No one knows, my darling. No one has the key."

"That's ridiculous," said Edward. "How can you have lost the key?"

"I didn't lose the key," she said. "It's just that no one has it."

Steam came out of Edward's ears. Dinner was served.

When Edward tasted the turkey he said it was underdone. He always said that. He could tell when he was carving it but nobody believed him. Fanny was annoyed. She said, "Then send it back."

Priscilla told Louellen such a long and involved story during dinner that Louellen couldn't even follow it. Louellen nodded and chewed, nodded and chewed. It was all she could do. She was beautiful anyhow, with her pink lips, her long neck. That was what Andrew was thinking across the table. And he was thinking of other things he'd like to be doing right at that moment. Things with Louellen. He stood up.

Louellen's moving in with me!

he said. There was a moment of silence, then all at once everybody started congratulating them. Fanny got up, draped her arms around Louellen, and kissed her, gravely, on the cheek. She sat down again, next to her daughter-in-law-to-be, making Priscilla move over. Fanny wanted to know whether Louellen had told her parents yet. Louellen said not yet. "No, of course not," Fanny said. "Of course you'd want to tell us first. Anyhow, your mother's going to be thrilled. Who could imagine a better catch than Andrew?"

"I hadn't thought of it exactly in that way," said Louellen.

It was a lie. She *had* thought of it in exactly that way, but in fact she had come to the opposite conclusion: that for a Berman of New Orleans, Andrew really wasn't a particularly good "catch." He didn't come from old money, and no one in his family was in the arts, nor were they intellectuals or even anything vaguely bohemian or interesting. He himself was broke, and he wasn't even really tall enough for her.

But she loved him nevertheless.

Little Mike proposed a toast and they all clinked glasses, even Pilar, because even though it was abundantly clear that she was uncomfortable, Fanny and Little Mike had insisted that she sit with the family at the Thanksgiving table.

Pilar jumped up long before dinner was over and started washing dishes. Then gradually everyone moved into the living room and Fanny started opening presents. She opened the ugly one from Andrew and Louellen and inside was a life-sized ceramic turkey from Italy. It was looking up with its beak open, prepared to die a turkey's watery death. Fanny loved it, and she said she didn't know they had turkeys in Italy (which got everybody thinking) and she hugged Andrew and then Louellen and she said to Louellen, "Welcome to the bosom of our family."

Fanny was proud of herself for saying this.

Priscilla gave Fanny a black lace negligee. Edward gave her a powder blue chenille bathrobe. (Fanny and Edward were always giving each other bathrobes. They went through them like Kleenexes.) Carmen gave her a crystal atomizer. Little Mike gave her two Nat King Cole albums that he didn't have in his own collection. Fanny said, "Little Mike, you shouldn't have," but she hugged him anyway. She hugged them all and she thought, "Yes. This is what it's all about."

They ate pie.

After pie no one was allowed to go home. Edward made them all sit in the den. They had to watch the videotape of last year's Thanksgiving dinner, at which all were present except Louellen, who was in New Orleans with her family instead. The videotape was two hours long and represented in real time the entire meal and gift-opening session. Priscilla excused herself and went into the guest bathroom and sat in the shower and cried.

Louellen imagined worse things that could be happening to her. Spontaneous combustion was one. An earthquake measuring 9.7 on the Richter scale was another. Nuclear war. Every time something "funny" happened on the tape, Edward or Little Mike rewound it and played it back again. "Louellen, look at this part. Watch this," they said. It was all ostensibly for Louellen's benefit. She should have been there. She should not have been in Louisiana with her own family, who asked her endless questions about "that Kelbow boy" and his intentions after dating their daughter for six full months. Andrew worried about Louellen having to sit there for so long when he knew she wanted to go home and have sex as badly as he did. Fanny was happy to watch the tape. She loved her family. The only parts she hated to watch were when she herself was on the screen. She thought she looked fat, old, and dumb.

Louellen walked over to the bathroom and knocked on the door. "Priscilla?" she said. "Are you okay?"

Priscilla reached over from the shower and unlocked the door. "Come in," she told Louellen. Louellen went in and sat facing Priscilla, cross-legged on the tiled shower floor. They talked about men while Edward and Little Mike watched last year's Thanksgiving on TV and Pilar cleaned the stove and Fanny and Andrew unloaded the dishwasher and put the clean dishes back into the green thing.

Thanksgiving Part II:
The Father's Turn

Friday afternoon Andrew and Louellen drove over to Don's for Thanksgiving dinner. It was a gray day; a shroud of fog smothered the city, and it started raining as Little Mike and Carmen rode over the hill on Little Mike's motorcycle. They were drenched by the time they arrived, and for this Little Mike blamed Don.

Don, however, didn't have any way of knowing that Little Mike was the least bit angry at him because Little Mike didn't show his anger at all. In fact, he never did. Perhaps Little Mike himself didn't even know he was angry. So that when Don invited Little Mike to a Lakers game on the following Tuesday, it wasn't because he was trying to mollify him. As he prepared to invite him, his eyes sparkled because he knew that what he had in his possession, Lakers tickets, was a real commodity. This was something he very much wanted to share with his younger son; he had the idea way in the back of his mind that the experience of the two of them going to a game together would deepen their relationship in some way. They'd have dinner first, early—maybe a steak—at a good restaurant, sizzling black and blue, and big glasses of bourbon on the rocks. "Mike," he said, and he turned to his son, who was blowing smoke rings at Valentina. "Tuesday night—are you busy? You want to go to the Lakers game with your old dad?"

"Who's playing?" said Little Mike.

"Detroit," said Don.

"Senate seats?" said Little Mike.

"I don't want to twist your arm," said Don, feeling a little deflated.

"It sounds great," Little Mike said. "You're on."

"Should be a great game," said Don. There was no conflict about not inviting Andrew, who was not, after all, a sports fan.

At about four-thirty Andrew and Little Mike went into the kitchen to rescue the turkey because Don persisted in overcooking it every year. In fact it was already overdone, so Andrew took it out of the oven. It was beautifully browned, but when Andrew stuck a fork in it, the juices not only didn't run clear, they didn't run at all.

Don came into the kitchen. "What are you doing?" he said. "I think it needs about another half hour."

"It's done," said Andrew. "How long has it been in?"

Don looked at his watch. "Five and a half hours," said Don.

"Too long," said Little Mike.

"But it's eighteen pounds."

"You never have to cook a turkey more than three hours and forty-five minutes no matter how big it is," said Little Mike, who had picked up a thing or two in the kitchen himself by now. He secretly thought he made better sauces than Andrew, favoring long-reduced veal stocks as bases. He had brought some demi-glace in a little jar from his own refrigerator to stir into the sauce he would make by throwing some shallots into the roasting pan, deglazing with cognac, and adding some chicken stock (canned would have to do, since Don wasn't the type of person who kept homemade stock in his freezer). The last step would be stirring in a spoonful of the demi-glace. At least the sauce would be gorgeous, even if the bird was overcooked.

"But it's huge," said Don.

"Three hours and forty-five minutes," said Andrew and Little Mike in unison.

"Really?" said Don. "Okay." But Andrew and Little Mike both knew that by this time next year he'd have completely forgotten about this conversation and he'd overcook it again. And so on every year.

Halfway through dinner Andrew said, "Dad? Why did you and Mom break up?" From out of nowhere.

"Well," said Don, and suddenly he had to admit to himself that the turkey was indeed a little dry. Everyone was looking at him. "I was going through a lot of changes, and your mother just wasn't interested in . . . progressing with me." That sounded satisfactory.

"Oh, really?" said Little Mike. "As I understand it, you were fucking your secretary."

"He was what?" said Valentina.

"Fucking his secretary," said Little Mike. "You oughtta have a little chat with my mom about it someday."

Valentina's daughters started tittering nervously.

"There was more to it than that," said Don.

"You're unbelievable," Andrew said to his brother. "Don't you owe Dad an apology?"

"I don't know. Do I?" Little Mike looked around at everyone, and no one was saying anything. "Dad," he said, "I'm sorry."

Don just looked at him.

"Well," said Andrew to his father, "I'd love to hear about it sometime if you ever feel like sitting down and talking about it."

"You're on," said Don. As fate would have it, however, Don would never get around to feeling like it.

Andrew and Louellen announced their moving-in-together to Don and Valentina after the other company had left, and Don was thrilled. It was as though he had already forgotten the extreme discomfort of the dinner conversation. A slow smile crept over his face. "You know," he said quietly, "the fact that you found Louellen, Andrew, and that Little Mike found Carmen is enough to prove the existence of God."

The Purple Dusk of Twilight Time

Priscilla called Fanny on Saturday afternoon. She wanted to invite Fanny and Edward to the Fox Venice to see the first four and a half hours of Rainer Werner Fassbinder's *Berlin Alexanderplatz.*

"I'd rather go stand naked on the corner of Sunset and Alvarado," said Fanny. "With guacamole smeared all over my body."

"Or we could do that," said Priscilla, but instead they chose another movie.

Edward said he didn't feel well, he thought that damn flu was coming back.

"I'll stay home and make you chicken soup," said Fanny.

"No," said Edward, "you go out with Priscilla and have a good time."

"If that's possible," Fanny added, and she kissed him goodbye and promised to make him chicken soup when she got home. As soon as Fanny left, Edward took all the dishes and linens out of the green thing. He tried to open door No. 3, but as usual, he had no luck. He even stuck his car key into the lock, but then worried about breaking the key.

Edward stacked all the Grandma dishes neatly on the dining room table, and then he got in his car and drove to Madeleine's Rent-a-Rig. Madeleine, an old broad with wild hair and a mustache, rented him a fourteen-foot minitruck because it was the smallest rig she had left. Edward parked his gleaming black BMW in Madeleine's lot and drove the minitruck home.

Little Mike was still sleeping even though it was two-thirty. Carmen was at work. Edward tried to wake up Little Mike. "Mike," he said softly, but his gentle voice didn't stand a chance of penetrating the heavy slumber of a nineteen-year-old boy who'd had too much to drink and too much to smoke and killer sex on top of it all for too many nights in a row. Edward slammed the bedroom door, but when he opened it again and looked in, Little Mike hadn't stirred. He stretched Little Mike's eyelids open with his fingers and put his face right up to Little Mike's. "Wake up!" he said loudly.

Little Mike's eyeballs rolled into view. "What do you want?" he said.

"Time to get up," said Edward. "I'd like you to help me with something."

A half hour later, Edward and Little Mike were driving in the minitruck over Laurel Canyon. The green thing, unanchored, was banging around in back.

When they arrived at Andrew's apartment on Sycamore, Edward rang the buzzer.

As it turned out Andrew and Louellen were both there, and

this was a fortunate thing for Edward because in his haste he hadn't called first. Louellen answered the intercom.

"It's Edward," said Edward.

Louellen activated the door buzzer and Little Mike propped open the door with a potted areca palm.

Luckily there were only three stairs leading up to the building entrance. A muscle sprang in Edward's back, but still he went on. He and Little Mike struggled to maneuver the green thing through the narrow doorway of Andrew's ground-floor apartment.

Louellen said, "Edward, what on God's earth are you doing with that?"

Edward said, "It's a moving-in-together present."

Louellen looked at Andrew, and he shrugged. Louellen said, "Well, thank you, Edward. I was telling Andrew just this morning that this place has been positively screamin' out for more furniture, and a brown sideboard in particular."

"I don't know where you're going to put it," said Little Mike, looking around. There were white Danish bookcases lining every wall, filled with classics that Andrew dimly remembered, and other books he'd never forget—cookbooks and classics of the modern theater and film—Harold Clurman's *On Directing*, Syd Fields's *Screenplay*, Marcella Hazan's *Classic Italian Cookbook*, *The Chez Panisse Cookbook*, and of course *Mastering the Art of French Cooking*, volumes I and II.

Edward collapsed on the sofa.

Then Don came out of the bathroom. He had been there all the time. Valentina had to go out of town to promote her book, *I'm a Right Brain, You're O.K.,* so Andrew had invited Don over for bagels and lox. Louellen looked at Edward expectantly. He stood up, startled, and the two men shook hands.

"Good to see you, Edward," said Don, and he grinned and clasped Edward's warm hand a moment longer than was comfortable. The last communication they had had was several years earlier, when Don was still paying child support for Little Mike. Edward blew up one month when Don was late with the check, and even called him a cocksucker in a moment of passionate fury. A few weeks later Don had gone to Washington State on business and he sent Edward a postcard with a picture of a volcano erupting, with the caption:

MT. ST. HELENS ERUPTS IN A
LAVA-SPEWING EXPLOSION!

and on the message side he wrote

Edward: I saw this and thought of you.
Love,
Don

Louellen offered Edward a mimosa, which he snatched rather hastily and drank down. Andrew began to worry that he was in for a quarrel with his beloved. Because he knew that Louellen wouldn't want to keep the green thing, but for them to refuse or give away such a generous gift from Fanny and Edward would be the moral equivalent of a sock in the jaw.

Edward said, "Hey, I'm sorry I don't have the key to the right-hand cabinet and I have no idea what's in there. You'll just have to live with it."

"It's a damn shame," said Louellen, "because Lord knows we could use the additional storage space." She rolled her eyes up into her head, but only Andrew saw this.

"I have the key," said Don.

"*You* have it?" Edward was astonished.

"I was wondering when someone was going to ask me for it."

"Where is it?" said Edward. "Do you know where it is?"

"It's in my pocket," said Don, patting his pants.

"You carry it with you?" said Little Mike.

"I've had it on my key ring for years," said Don.

"Well?" said Edward.

"Well, what?" said Don.

Little Mike kept looking back and forth between his two fathers, excited by the possibility of confrontation.

"Can I have it?" said Edward. He was getting impatient.

"Oh, you want me to *give* it to you?" said Don.

"Look, Don," said Edward. "I'm getting impatient. Please let me have the key."

Louellen whispered in Andrew's ear, "Do something, for cryin' out loud." But Andrew was transfixed.

"How much is it worth to you?" said Don.

Little Mike said, "Dad, let him have the key."

Don turned slowly to Little Mike. "You think I should just *give* it to him?" The corner of Don's mouth was curled up in something like a smile.

"Dad, what's wrong with you?" said Little Mike.

"Fifty dollars," said Don to Edward.

"Fifty dollars?" said Edward.

"Do you want it or not?" said Don. "Come on. Let's do business." Don thought this was funny, and maybe it was, or maybe later on they might look back on it and think it was; no one was sure.

"This is ridiculous," said Edward. He looked around the room, unsure of what to do. "I'll give you twenty," he said finally.

"Forty."

"Forget it," said Edward. "This is so stupid."

"How would everyone like another mimosa?" said Louellen, and she went into the kitchen.

Edward started toward the door. "I don't have to take this," he said. But he stopped. He wanted to put the matter to rest. He had to know what was in door No. 3. He turned around. "My final offer," he said to Don. "Twenty-five."

"Thirty-five and you've got a deal," said Don.

"Forget it," said Edward.

Don said, "Edward, I can't believe ten dollars means that much to you. I take it business isn't too good lately?"

"Thirty bucks," said Edward.

"Sold!"

Edward whipped out his checkbook, started writing a check. "I don't have much cash," he said.

Don said, "Can I see two pieces of I.D.?"

Edward threw him a look. "You'll just have to trust me, Don," he said. Then, under his breath, "Asshole."

Don folded the check in half and put it in his wallet. Then he took a small, luggage-type key off the key ring and gave it to Edward, bowing ceremoniously.

Edward fit the key into door No. 3 of the green thing. He turned the key, opened the door. Inside: a large gray-green hollow plastic owl that Don and Fanny used to hang on a low branch of the rubber tree in the backyard of the house in the valley to scare away the mockingbird who kept young Don and his wife awake night after night, not because of the loudness of the song but because of its miraculous variety.

"What is it?" said Edward.

Louellen pulled it out and set it on the coffee table.

Don burst out laughing. His was a violent storm of laughter. It was Mount Saint Helens erupting in a lava-spewing explosion. It was an earthquake, a squall, a belly laugh. It was the best laugh Don had had in years.

Edward stared at the hysterical man in Andrew's apartment, and Little Mike and Andrew waited for the aftershocks. Louellen stepped up to Edward and said softly in his ear, "You've got to admit, Edward, it is pretty funny." And soon Edward allowed himself a chuckle. Then another, and soon they were all laughing. Edward stood and picked up the weightless owl and spontaneously drop-kicked it to a far corner of the ceiling. It landed upside down, on its head, in a basket of *American Film* magazines and *Daily Variety*s, and Little Mike took it out of the basket and set it upright on top of the green thing. All quiet, the extended family looked at the owl for a moment.

At last Edward said, "Don, I'm going to stop payment on that check."

And Don laughed even harder, if that's possible, and made a show of tearing up the check, scattering the little pieces on the carpet like rice at a wedding.

Fabulous Forum

On Tuesday evening, Little Mike was supposed to meet Don at Bob Burn's Steakhouse at the end of Wilshire Boulevard in Santa Monica; when Don arrived, the sun was setting violet and orange over the ocean. Little Mike was late.

When it had been a half hour, Don motioned to the waitress. He was sitting in a booth near the piano bar, but it was still too early for music. The waitress came over, and Don said, "Well, my son's very late, and we're going to the Lakers game. So I'm going to go ahead and order for both of us." He ordered himself a filet, medium rare, and a porterhouse for Little Mike, black and blue. Caesar salad for both, and a bottle of cabernet.

When Don was just finishing up, his face hardened into an expression of anger and hurt, Little Mike came into the restaurant, flushed and cheerful. "Sorry," he said. "I ran out of gas." Don could barely speak. They had Little Mike's steak wrapped up to go.

The Lakers lost to the Pistons, 121–109.

Takanawa Landscapes

In June, Pilar worked in the garden. She raked the fallen blossoms from under the jacaranda tree because even though they were a beautiful color of blue, they made the whole yard smell like pee-pee. The hollyhocks, as tall as Ken, stood out next to the house, saturated pink against the stark white stucco. Pilar sat on the stone path and began to weed the vegetable bed. The lettuce, red-leafed, neglected for weeks, was growing into tall stalks and blossoming; it would be too bitter now to eat. But the tomatoes were perfect; she bit into one: it was dark red and bursting with the flavor of twenty tomatoes.

Ken pulled into the driveway in the small white pickup truck that said TAKANAWA LANDSCAPES. "Are you weeding?" he said, slamming the door as he got out of the pickup. "That's good." He kissed Pilar's cheek and sat next to her on the path of flagstones he had laid when they first moved in. He pulled a few weeds, tasted a tomato. "So good this year," he said. "Let's have tomato salad."

Pilar could tell that her husband wanted to talk about something. "What is it, *corazón?*" she said. "Tell me who died."

"No," he said. "Nobody died. My mother is going to come to visit."

Pilar had never met Ken's ancient mother, who lived in Osaka and who had never once visited her son in the United States since he left Japan in 1949.

"We will have to replant these beds," said Ken. "I'll get my boys over and we'll plant the shade beds too." He gestured broadly over to the far fence.

"And the house," said Pilar. "I'll have to do some things."

"I want her to feel she's at home," said Ken.

Pilar said, "Yes, I'll make some new curtains for the extra bedroom and we'll get a new bedspread." Pilar was nervous to meet Ken's mother. She spoke not a word of English or Spanish, and Pilar spoke only a few words of Japanese. *Do itasimasite,* she could say, and *ohayo gozaimasu.* Beyond that, all she really knew were the tongue twisters Ken had taught her, including

> *Nama mugi, nama gome, nama tamago*
> *Nama mugi, nama gome, nama tamago*

which she could say very fast, faster even than her husband. But what could she say to the mother of Ken? What if she asked about their childlessness? Tongue twisters would explain nothing. Maybe she could make her believe Little Mike was their son. He was the right age. Was he dark enough? She tried to picture Ken as a father, which was hard because she couldn't even picture him as a son.

Fanny's Choice

It was the finals, the Lakers against the Celts, and Andrew was trying to get into basketball. "If you can't get into *this*," Little Mike said, "you're just an antisports geek."

"Looks like I'm an antisports geek," Andrew said at the half. He and Carmen and Fanny started doing the dishes while Edward and Little Mike retired to the den with their big plates of strawberry shortcake to watch the second half. "This is not basketball food," said Edward. "It's too messy." The Lakers were up six points in Boston Garden, a hell of a game.

Andrew said, "Okay, Mom. Let's play 'Fanny's Choice.'"

"How do you play?" said Fanny.

"Little Mike and I fall out of a boat in very rough seas. We're both drowning, but you can only save one of us. Who do you save?"

"Oh, Andrew, you're so weird," said Carmen.

"I save you both," said Fanny, turning on the garbage disposal.

Carmen started stuffing salad greens down it with her hand. Fanny pulled Carmen's hand out of the sink and slapped it.

"You don't understand the game," said Andrew. "You can only save *one* of us. You have to choose."

"No, I don't," said Fanny. "I don't *have* to do anything."

"Okay," said Andrew. "Let's try another one. We're in a concentration camp. The Nazis are going to send me or Little Mike to the oven, but *you're* the one who has to decide, or else we both go."

"I tell them I'll go instead."

"They're Nazis, Mom. They won't listen to reason. They're animals. So who do you choose?"

Fanny said, "Carmen, tell him to leave me alone."

"Leave her alone," said Carmen.

Andrew's game was even more insidious than it sounded because he knew that deep in Fanny's heart, she preferred him to Little Mike. Torturing his mother in this way amused Andrew— he told himself it was harmless fun.

A roar came up from the den.

"What happened?" shouted Fanny, and she ran into the den, rubbing her soapy hands on her jeans.

"Magic just made an unbelievable three-pointer with one second on the shot clock, and the Celts can't hit the boards to save their lives."

"Yay!" said Fanny, ducking back into the kitchen. She was very upset. If she *really* had to choose, she knew she would choose Andrew. But she felt so badly about it that she decided she would have to choose Little Mike instead, just to prove that she loved her children equally; plus, she couldn't stand the guilt of choosing the one that was really her favorite. But then people might think that she loved Little Mike more than Andrew, and that would be dreadful too, and on top of everything else, Andrew would be dead.

The guilt would be unbearable either way. She couldn't win. She would have to kill herself. And if it meant taking both her children with her in order not to be forced, so be it.

She said to Carmen, "Never have children."

Off and Running

By this time, Little Mike had become a truly *great* phone sales-man. He was making major dough. Six or seven hundred bucks a week, if the majority of his orders confirmed. Not to mention if *all* of them confirmed; then he'd really rake. And as horrible as it was to drag himself out of bed at five-thirty in the morning to be there at six, the beautiful part was that he was finished by noon—early enough to make the Daily Double at Hollywood Park.

Friday was payday, and Little Mike stopped at the bank and cashed his paycheck on the way to the track—four hundred and seventy-five bucks after taxes. He deposited a hundred and seventy-five and put three hundred—six brand-new fifties—in his pocket.

Little Mike always had a gin and tonic between the sixth and seventh races: it seemed to bring him good luck. Sometimes Sam bought him one. Sam was his racetrack buddy, an old guy who wore a plaid seersucker jacket year-round. The jacket reminded Little Mike of one his father used to have a long time ago, a blue-and-white-striped number that Don used to call his "happy jacket."

"Winner buys," said Sam, handing Little Mike his gin and tonic. "How'd you do?"

"I hate this track," said Little Mike, grinning. "The planes come in so low they scare the shit out of the horses."

"How much did you lose?" said Sam.

"On that race? Fifty bucks. Give me Santa Anita any day of the week."

"Listen, kid," said Sam, putting his arm around Little Mike's shoulder. "I think you're putting too much emphasis on speed rating. It's just a number, you know what I mean? Just a number. Past performance is the ticket. Look at how the horses like to run. I mean, what's an eighty-nine speed rating if a horse likes to run second? You know what I mean? Past performance. Now *that's* what I mean by classical handicapping."

"Who do you like in the seventh?" said Little Mike, ordering another round.

After much discussion, he wound up putting forty dollars on the nose of an Irish filly, Unforgettable. And he wasn't just betting on the name either—this horse had *potential.* She looked terrific two races ago, but faltered at the gate on her last start with a nobody jockey aboard. This time, Lafitte Pincay was riding. Unforgettable was due.

She looked gorgeous when they walked her around the track before the race; she looked ready. At the last minute Little Mike went back to the window and baseballed her on the exacta, stopping at the bar for another G & T; he came back outside and took a seat down in front of the rail just as the horses were locked into the starting gate. He felt good.

The flag went up and the horses flew out of the gate—a full field of twelve. Unforgettable had excellent post position—fourth—and she broke nicely. In fact, she looked good all the way through, taking the inside on the curve. But then in the stretch, a horse came out of nowhere—who was it? the No. 6 horse? and, amazingly, pulled out far ahead of the field to win. It was Bold Determination with Angel Cordero, by four or five lengths.

Unforgettable placed.

By the end of the day, Little Mike had lost two hundred and eighty dollars, leaving only a twenty in his pocket. He bought himself another gin and tonic as a consolation (they never carded him at the track), but then he decided to leave before the ninth race, and try to miss some of the traffic.

The San Diego Freeway was a nightmare, and it was only four-thirty. Traffic stood virtually at a standstill in the fast lane. It would take him an hour to get home. Little Mike reached under the passenger seat to find his shoe box full of cassettes, but it was jammed underneath. As he was trying to free it, his foot slipped off the clutch, his car lurched forward, he felt a sharp thud. All at once he realized he had rear-ended the car in front of him.

It was a Mercedes. Maybe five years old. It pulled over into the emergency lane next to the center divider, and Little Mike followed. The woman driving got out, all pissed off.

Little Mike got out too. "Sorry," he said, and went to look for damage to her car.

"What the hell were you doing?" she said. "I don't suppose you have insurance, either, right?" She was a small, angry bleached-blonde, wearing a large white stretchy outfit and slip-on Keds.

"I have insurance," he said. "Relax."

Fortunately he had only scratched her bumper.

"Look," he said. "It's nothing. Are you okay?"

She was rubbing her back, and he hoped she wasn't the whiplash type. "I think so," she said. "But you better give me your information just in case."

Little Mike went back and rummaged around his glove compartment until he found his insurance certificate. He tried to remember the last time he paid the bill.

"I didn't hit you very hard," he said when he handed her the papers. "I couldn't have been going more than two miles an hour."

"Yeah yeah yeah," she said. "I'm probably okay." But she wrote down all the information anyway.

Where've you been?" said Fanny when Little Mike finally got home. Fanny and Carmen were drinking white wine in the kitchen.

"Hollywood Park," he said.

"Oh, fun," said Carmen. "How'd you do?"

"I won," he said.

"Yay!" said Fanny. "How much?"

"Two hundred bucks."

"That's great," said Carmen. "You'll have to take me out and celebrate."

"We'll go out this weekend," said Little Mike.

"Joe came by," said Fanny. "He was sitting in the driveway when I came home."

"Did you talk to him?"

"He wants you to call him right away," said Fanny.

Little Mike went off toward his bedroom.

"Do you owe him money?" shouted Fanny. Little Mike ignored her.

Little Mike lay on his bed and did a bong hit. He owed Joe a hundred and forty dollars, but at least he had enough pot to last him the rest of the week. He picked up the phone to call Joe, but there was no dial tone.

Carmen appeared in the doorway. "You told me you took care of the phone bill," she said.

"I thought I had."

"You thought . . . ?"

"Come here, sweetheart," said Little Mike. "Sshhh . . ." And his dimples were so cute that Carmen came and lay next to him, and Little Mike wrapped his arms around her and kissed her lovely shoulders and the nape of her neck until she squirmed and giggled.

"What are you going to do about money?" she said after a while.

"I'm going to do what any normal, red-blooded American boy would do in my situation," he said.

"What's that?" said Carmen.

"Ask my dad for a loan."

Lunch with Father

Don took such matters as loans to his son very seriously: he met Little Mike for lunch on a weekday to hear his request.

"What is the money for?" said Don, looking down through his reading glasses at Little Mike. They were in Harry's Bar in Century City, and Don was in entertainment-lawyer mode in crisp shirt and expensive Italian suit; he exchanged greetings with nine-tenths of the men in the restaurant, well-dressed middle-aged attorneys and baby-faced C.A.A. agents. Since the time Don had quit the prestigious law firm twelve years before, he had slowly built up a very successful private practice, specializing in film contracts. His clients were major players—more often producers and directors than stars—and he put together the packages.

"I need to clear up some debts," said Little Mike. "I want to clean up my act."

"You really do?" said Don, after deciding what to order. He

looked Little Mike directly in the eyes. "How do I know you're not going to fuck up?" Little Mike had borrowed money from him several times before, and never paid him back.

"Because I'm telling you I'm not," said Little Mike.

Don looked back at his menu for another moment, then closed it and set it down on the table. "Why is this time different from every other time?" he said.

"Because I've been doing a lot of thinking about my life," said Little Mike, looking down. "And I've decided I don't want to fuck up anymore."

Don left him in suspense while they ordered lunch. Don ordered a *tricolore* seafood salad; Little Mike ordered carpaccio to start, then a veal chop. They both drank Pellegrino water, no ice.

"Okay," said Don when the waiter went away. "I'm willing to loan you one thousand dollars. Five percent interest, and I want it back in full in one year." He had never asked for interest before, and never set a deadline for repayment.

"Great," said Little Mike. "I really, really appreciate it." It was the perfect show-business lunch.

The next day Fanny and Edward's phone rang and Little Mike answered it.

It was Don. "Your phone is out of order," he said.

"I know," said Little Mike. "They're working on the lines."

"Listen," said Don. "I discussed with Valentina the idea of making you that loan, and she didn't feel very good about it."

"What are you talking about?" said Little Mike. "*You* sure seemed to feel pretty good about it yesterday."

"She's my wife," said Don quietly.

"Fuck your wife; I'm your son," said Little Mike.

"I'm sorry," said Don. "I really am. But that's the way it is. You're going to have to figure out something else."

"Right," said Little Mike. "Like what, for instance?"

"Why don't you ask Edward and Fanny?"

"I can't fucking believe you," said Little Mike. "You *said* you'd make me the loan."

"Mike," said Don. "You seem to think the world owes you something. Well, it doesn't."

"Thanks a lot," said Little Mike. He hung up on his father and decided never to speak to him again.

Serpent's Tooth

Don had a sudden attack of colitis brought on by the Crohn's disease that hadn't bothered him once since it sent him to the hospital in 1968; this time he wound up in intensive care at Cedars. The gastroenterologist took apart Don's intestine, resectioned it, and unhooked it, and when Don woke up, the good-looking young doctor told him that wearing his new ostomy bag might negatively affect his body image, but he assured Don that in a few months he'd be completely accustomed to it. However, he warned him that in the future he must find a way to relax or the colitis would come back.

Fanny sent Don flowers in the hospital, and she wanted Little Mike to visit him. Carmen and Andrew had gone together while Don was still in intensive care, but Little Mike still refused to speak to him, even now that he was in a room.

"I'm not going," Little Mike said. "He's an asshole."

Fanny said, "He may be an asshole, but he's your father." She was very proud of herself for taking this generous stance, and very disappointed in Little Mike.

Finally he agreed to go but not if Valentina was going to be there at the same time.

"I could have died," said Don when his son finally came. "I could have died with you angry at me," and at that point Little Mike began to sob uncontrollably. After that he tried to forgive his father.

She Mustered the Courage

Fanny tried to fire Pilar for weeks, unsuccessfully. Even thinking about it gave her a terrible stomachache.

Finally she mustered the courage.

"Pilar," she said.

Pilar looked up. "Mrs. Kelbow," Pilar said sadly (this was the form her advancing years took: sadness). Fanny looked at her, hoping she was about to quit. Her heart was pounding, pounding, pounding. "Mrs. Kelbow?" said Pilar. "When you gonna get a new vacuum cleaner?"

Fanny clutched the front of her blouse. "This week," she mumbled down into her chest. "This week, Pilar. I promise."

Fanny fired her the next week. She told Pilar that she was quitting her job in order to stay at home, so she no longer needed a cleaning lady.

Pilar hugged Fanny then, and Fanny started weeping.

"I'm so happy for you," said Pilar. "I know how much you hate to work."

Pilar was right about that. Fanny managed to pull into the garage every evening at exactly 5:32; when the clock in her office hit 5:00 she was out of there like the cork out of a bottle of champagne.

So Fanny fired Pilar, and from that day on and for the rest of her life, she suffered a little pang each and every Wednesday morning.

Ken's Ancient Mother

Ken's ancient mother was coming from Japan, and Pilar was worried. The house looked very good; Pilar had cleaned it the way she never cleaned her own house before. It was August: Maria's corn stand had the very fresh corn, and Pilar was planning to make green corn tamales. Lupe and her husband and their children, a teenage boy and girl, Pilar's niece and nephew, were coming over to the house on Saturday afternoon, and also Hiro Shimpo, Ken's right-hand man at the nursery for the last ten years; they'd all be there when Pilar and Ken got back from the airport. Pilar thought it best to have a lot of people there; with lots of family, there would not be so many awkward silences.

"I want her to feel at home," said Ken on Thursday night. "You'll have to go over to the Japanese grocery stores on Sawtelle tomorrow and get her some things." Pilar was only working four days a week now that she no longer had Mrs. Kelbow; she had time to prepare.

Pilar was quiet. It wasn't that she was afraid to drive, but out of the valley she felt lost, and she didn't know what turns to make off the freeway to get to the Japanese grocery stores. "Maybe because she's coming to a new country, she'd like to try some Mexican food." Pilar knew a lot of Americans who had never even tried green corn tamales.

"It won't kill you to pick up some stuff for her," said Ken. "Some *misoshiro*, some pickled cabbage and tofu. You can make Mexican food or whatever you want on Saturday, but I want to have some stuff around the house that she'll want to eat."

"We can go on the way to the airport on Saturday," said Pilar. "Isn't it on the way?"

"I want her to feel we've prepared for her visit," said Ken. "Can't you just do me a favor, and make her feel welcome?"

Pilar did drive over the hill the next day, carefully following Ken's exact directions, and although the freeway was terrifying, she stayed in the slow lane and found her exit. She kept driving for a while on Santa Monica Boulevard, and it was funny because she thought Sawtelle would come right away, but soon everything was unfamiliar. Pilar didn't know how many miles she drove in a straight line on Santa Monica Boulevard, but finally the street ended, and it felt like she was at the end of the world. She got out of her car and looked, and she was looking out over the ocean. This was called Ocean Avenue. The city ended here, with a tall white stone statue of the beautiful Santa Monica with her back to the ocean, and there were steep cliffs, and far below, the beaches. It was foggy here, and damp, and cool, even though it was a hundred degrees in the valley—dry, desert heat. Goose pimples rose on Pilar's arm as she looked out across the ocean to the horizon, trying to imagine Japan.

~~~

Later, Pilar found Sawtelle Avenue, and she felt very stupid because it was only two blocks from the freeway exit. She picked up all the things Ken had told her to buy, plus a bag of tiny silver dried fish, with their heads left on and their tiny solid white eyes, and a bag of roasted green peas, each with a crust of wasabi, and a long, white radish called daikon, a box of bonito stock, and some rubbery, bright pink-and-white fishcakes. Even the nori looked fresher than she could ever find at Gelson's.

On Saturday, Pilar and Ken drove to the airport, and they waited at the baggage claim for Ken's ancient mother to come out of customs. Ken was very quiet.

When the tiny woman emerged from the customs area, Pilar could tell immediately that it was Ken's ancient mother, although she didn't look very ancient. She looked maybe sixty-five. She looked just like Ken, but with bad posture. Pilar may have recognized her before Ken did.

Pilar found it surprising that after forty years, Ken did not even kiss his mother, although he told her later that Japanese people rarely kiss each other. That was something she never knew, for Ken kissed her often enough. Ken took his mother's hand and squeezed it, as though she were an honored business associate. He called her "Mama-San."

Mama-San actually seemed to enjoy herself on Saturday evening, and she sampled all of the different Mexican dishes Pilar had made. She seemed to particularly like the green corn tamales, sweet corn pudding with a little queso fresco in the center, steamed in the green husks. It was beautiful in the backyard, with the garden all lush in August and the tomatoes bursting on the vine, and they ate Pilar's delicious Mexican food sitting at a redwood table under the jacaranda tree. Hiro Shimpo was very good about translating between Mama-San and the rest of the company when Ken was busy, and Pilar's family, especially her niece, seemed to be fascinated by the old lady.

By the time it started getting dark, Pilar could see that Mama-San was exhausted. She came and took Mama-San's arm and told Ken to tell Mama-San she was going to take her to her bedroom, and Pilar felt better than she had felt in a long time, because now she had someone to take care of.

Eat It and Archie

Eighteen months passed with the length of eighteen winters. Long for Fanny because during this interval came the series of Salvadoran ladies. The first one was Maria, and she did a terrific job cleaning Fanny's house; everything sparkled. But the following Tuesday (yes, to Fanny's chagrin, cleaning day was no longer Wednesday but Tuesday) it was not Maria who showed up, but Marta, her fat cousin. The next month it was Luisa, Marta's mother, and then a tall thin seemingly unrelated woman named Olivia.

"I can't stand this," said Fanny. "It's like a Cinco de Mayo parade."

"Cinco de Mayo is Mexican, Mom, not Salvadoran," said Little Mike.

"Oh, really, smarty-pants? You mean one day it's May fourth and the next it's May sixth unless you're in Mexico?"

"El Salvador is not Mexico," said Little Mike.

"Yes, it is," said Fanny. "Only more so."

"I can't even talk to you," said Little Mike.

Fanny looked very sad. "I want Pilar back," she said.

"I knew it," said Edward.

"Big deal, we all knew it," said Little Mike. "We knew you'd go crawling back to her on your hands and knees, pleading with her to return."

"I love Pilar," said Carmen. "Maybe if you ask her to come back she'll do a better job now."

"That's ridiculous," said Edward. "Why should she?"

"Because she misses us, that's why," said Fanny.

Fanny called Pilar and made up a story about having to go back to work half-time after all, which actually was true, and said she wanted Pilar to come back. But Pilar said no, she couldn't come back, she was retiring, and now she'd be very busy taking care of Ken's mother, who was staying forever in their house, and she told Fanny she had been relieved that Fanny fired her in the first place so she wouldn't have to disappoint her by quitting.

The next to come to the house were Edith and Arturo, Luisa's daughter-in-law and son. Their English was worse than Pilar's, but they cleaned the house in double-time. The stream of cleaning people ended here with Edith, who pronounced her name "Eat It," and Arturo, whom Fanny thought was shell-shocked from the civil war in El Salvador because he barely spoke a word. Fanny called them Edith and Archie behind their backs, and wondered where a Salvadoran woman got a name like Edith. One day she asked her. Edith was demure. She looked up at Fanny. "Eat It?" she said. With her everything sounded like a question. "Eat It? It was the name of the mother? Of my father?"

Fanny did not know this until years later, but back in Salvador Edith had been a well-paid legal secretary and Arturo was a university professor who taught organic chemistry. He was not shell-shocked, just quiet from hating having to leave his country, hating having to come to the United States, and hating having to pretend to like it. In the afternoons Edith and Arturo worked at the Beverly Hills Hotel changing the linens of the very rich.

Edith and Arturo cleaned the house until it was cleaner than it had ever been in the time of Pilar. But the real reason Fanny liked them so much was that Arturo loved Otto.

The Wedding Dress

Louellen stood at the stove frying hamburgers in her wedding dress. The stove was a large old Wedgewood model, one with a griddle in the middle of four burners, and though Louellen did not love to cook, she loved to use this griddle. She loved to pour pancake batter on it and watch it bubble up in hot oil; she loved to scramble eggs on it. And the half-inch-thick steel came so clean. There was a little drawer beneath the griddle for melting butter, and she always melted butter for Andrew in the drawer when she made him pancakes, and she gave him the melted butter in a tiny white porcelain pitcher, just the right thing.

It was just the right thing too for Andrew to marry her, which is why she stood frying hamburgers in her wedding dress. Andrew had never proposed. He also hadn't worked in months. Little Mike had proposed to Carmen already, and their wedding was planned for August in Malibu, at Carmen's father's beach house.

Louellen refused to suffer the indignity of proposing to

Andrew herself, which is what her friend Tina suggested she do when she came over to join Louellen for hamburgers that evening. Andrew had gone to dinner at Fanny's, and Louellen had instructed Andrew to tell Fanny she was sick in bed, because she didn't want to go.

The previous Sunday when Louellen and Andrew had gone to Fanny and Edward's for dinner, Little Mike and Carmen announced their engagement. This made Andrew so anxious that he put mashed potatoes all over his face and shaved them off with a butter knife. His family, Fanny and Edward and Carmen and Little Mike, did not react as if anything out of the ordinary had happened. Carmen simply handed him her napkin after everyone had stopped laughing, and Fanny said, "Oh, Andrew, you're such a wag."

Darn straight, Andrew should be nervous. Clearly he knew that what was right and proper was that he should have been announcing *their* engagement—his and Louellen's. How she hated him sometimes for not having the wherewithal to know what he really wanted out of life.

The wedding-dress thing was beyond Andrew's comprehension. "I just don't get it," he said at first, and Louellen explained that she simply wanted to wear a wedding dress at some point in her life and right now it didn't look like she'd ever get the chance unless she took the bull by the horns and just started wearing one. He tried not to mention it again.

One day after work at the foley stage, Louellen had gone to Neiman-Marcus in Beverly Hills and looked at wedding dresses. She was a woman who could decide things easily, and after a short hour and a half of try-ons and fittings, accompanied by imaginative descriptions to the saleslady about the details of the wedding, she had made her selection and paid for the full-length silk lace dress with money from her trust fund. Several weeks later, when it was ready, she was excited to bring it home, but when she showed it to Andrew, he still didn't propose. So Louellen took to wearing the dress whenever she was at home. When she came home from work or from running errands on a Saturday, she would change into it directly, and once she even slept in it. She often wore it around the apartment without shoes, and as a result the white hem was turning black.

The worst times for Andrew were when Louellen insisted on wearing it when they had friends over for dinner; Louellen would say nothing about it and Andrew had great difficulty explaining it all.

As Louellen flipped the burgers and Tina excused herself to call her husband, Louellen thought about her life. Her film, now finished for over a year, must get distribution. She must quit her job at the foley stage slamming car doors and punching turkey carcasses, and write another script. She must marry Andrew, whom she loved and cherished and longed for desperately, even when he was right there, next to her, in bed, asleep.

Protection

One night Edward had to work late, Carmen was out with her mother, Little Mike was who knows where, and Fanny spent the evening snuggled into the sofa with a bowl of bananas, sour cream, and sugar and Stephen King's *Pet Sematary*. The phone rang, and Fanny jumped three feet off the sofa. Otto blinked and looked concerned for a moment, then went back to sleep. Fanny thought it would be Edward saying he was on his way home, but when she answered it, it was Little Mike.

"Where are you?" she said. There was a lot of background noise.

"I need you to bail me out. I'm in jail." His voice sounded strangled, almost.

"What happened?" said Fanny. "Are you okay?"

"I got pulled over for some stupid broken taillight, and it turns out they had a warrant."

"What do I have to do?" said Fanny.

"Do you have cash?" said Little Mike. "They want four hundred and sixty-five dollars."

"Jesus Christ," said Fanny. "What was the warrant for?"

"Speeding," he said. "Actually it was two warrants. From a really long time ago."

"I'll have to stop at the cash machine," said Fanny. "I want you to know I'm furious."

"I'm sorry," said Little Mike.

"Where do I bring it?" she said.

"Hold on a second," said Little Mike, and he put the arresting officer on the phone, Officer Vargas.

"Vargas," he said.

"This is his mother," said Fanny. "What happened?"

"Oh, I wouldn't worry about it too much—kind of thing that could happen to anybody. He was swerving a little on Sepulveda Boulevard, just north of Victory, and I pulled him over for a taillight. I didn't want to give him a Breathalyzer, 'cause he's so young and everything and he seems like such a nice kid—just a little confused. Anyway, I ran the routine check on his driver's license, which, by the way, is expired, and it turns out he has two warrants, one from Palmdale and one from Newport Beach. Speeding. I told him, Look, you've gotta take care of these things, these things don't just go away. One of the warrants was two years old. I'm pretty sure he learned his lesson."

"Well, I hope so," said Fanny.

"Don't you worry about him," he said, "we're just sitting here shooting the dirt." And then he told her where to bring the money.

When Fanny got to the Van Nuys jailhouse, she paid the money at the desk, and she had to wait, seated in a row of dirty orange plastic chairs, for almost an hour.

Finally they brought out Little Mike.

"That was *horrible*," he said.

Fanny didn't say anything; she was too angry. She simply got up and started out the door ahead of Little Mike.

Silently, they got into Fanny's car.

After a while, Fanny said, "I expect you to pay me back every penny of that money."

"Of course," said Little Mike.

They drove for a while.

"They chained me to this real ugly guy on drugs," said Little Mike when they got home. "He looked like a gorilla and he kept drooling on my foot."

Fanny laughed. "Good," she said. "I hope you learned your lesson."

"Believe me," said Little Mike.

"Listen," said Fanny. "I think it would be best for everyone if we don't mention this to Edward."

Little Mike agreed, and wondered how he was going to break it to Carmen.

The only person Fanny told about it was Priscilla, and Priscilla thought it represented a serious problem and that Little Mike needed therapy. "Would you like me to ask my shrink for a referral?" she said.

"Yes," said Fanny. "Absolutely. I think it's a good idea."

The next day Priscilla (she was in analysis, four days a week) mentioned it to Linda. Linda thought about it for a moment and started to suggest someone she thought would be good, but then she stopped herself. "I think," she said, "it would be more appropriate for help to come from his father. That's where the conflict is."

"Well, he calls me 'Dad,'" said Priscilla. "Isn't that close enough?"

Meanwhile, Don was hosting a reception in his condo for the Dalai Lama that weekend, and Valentina was up in Marin County attending a seminar on "Getting in Touch with Your Dark Side."

"She could *teach* that one," said Little Mike. "I think she's wasting your money."

Fanny figured she'd better call Don and tell him about Little Mike's arrest, but it would be strange to tell Don about it and not tell Edward. She called Andrew instead and told him.

Andrew was very quiet. "That's terrible," he said finally. "What are you going to do?"

Fanny said, "Put off thinking about it as long as possible."

Soon after that, Little Mike made a killing at the track. Sam gave him a good tip on a gelding they'd been holding back in maiden races, and Little Mike bet a hundred dollars on him to win. The horse came in at six to one, and Little Mike made enough money to pay Fanny back, although he still had to appear in court and would probably have to pay a monster fine.

"I don't know," said Fanny later to Andrew. "I think he's getting better. He's not smoking as much dope, and he paid me back right away."

"Yeah," said Andrew, "but he made the money at the track."

"The point is," said Fanny, "he's trying."

Inventory

When Andrew finally got around to making duck, it killed a woman.

It had been a bad idea from the start because even though he found a promising recipe in the *New York Times Magazine*, Andrew had never made duck before, and impressing the husband-and-wife producing team of JoAnn and Dan McMann was essential to the fledgling comedy-writing careers of both Andrew and Louellen. However, not only did Andrew not favorably impress them, but he gave JoAnn a case of botulism and killed her dead. The gravity of the event caused Andrew to stop and take inventory of his life.

He had been with Louellen for almost four years. Louellen had finally stopped wearing her wedding dress around the apartment; she'd had it cleaned and put in storage, although the tattered lace around the hem needed some repairing. But Andrew knew Louellen too well to imagine that she had given up on the idea of marriage.

Louellen was still a foley artist, and she had an impressive repertoire of anything anyone might need: soft footfalls, windy nights, tinkling crystal chandeliers. She had that great Jewish-Southern sense of humor, a taste for adventure, a lovely New Orleans accent. She had fabulous legs, common sense, a modest trust fund.

And what did Andrew have? A bachelor's degree in English, a worthless master's degree in film, an enormous student-loan debt, a large unpaid MasterCard balance, and eighteen or nineteen extra pounds on his gut. This wasn't because he was neurotic or compulsive or necessarily had fat genes (though Fanny was no Jack Sprat), but because he truly understood food. Andrew found nothing wrong with being slightly overweight as long as it was for the right reason. Which it was. He loved food. He had a handsome face. He looked more like Edward than either of his parents. Dark hair, good forehead, deep-set, searching eyes. He could have been a young Monty Clift, in spite of the paunch. Louellen said Andrew had to lose twenty pounds or else gain thirty. If he lost twenty he'd be gorgeous enough to make it in show business, and if he gained thirty he'd have the *heft* to make it in show business. Throw his weight around, that sort of thing. Louellen, bless her heart, said she didn't care a straw which it would be, as long as he committed one way or the other, but really they had to do *something* to get their directing careers off the ground. If that meant writing screenplays first, which someone else would direct, and then eventually writing their own, which they would direct, so be it. So be it.

Meanwhile, JoAnn and Dan McMann weren't even in film; they were in television. They were two of the producers of *The Plodniks of Laguna*, the number two comedy on the number one

network. Seven or eight months earlier, when Andrew had gotten the idea that he and Louellen would be a perfect comedy-
writing team, they had sat down in front of the TV and started
watching shows. *The Plodniks*, part of the network's boffo
Wednesday night lineup, did make them laugh, and the show
had the reputation in Hollywood for having the best writing
in television, which was the only reason Andrew and Louellen
thought of writing for it. So Andrew and Louellen wrote a script
for *The Plodniks* on spec, and when they were satisfied that it
was reasonably hilarious, Andrew brought it over to the show's
casting director, the sister of a friend from film school. She loved
it and gave it to JoAnn and Dan McMann. Andrew and Louellen
had met the McManns once at a party, and they had all made
noises about getting together sometime, so this was perfect.
When the McManns finally got around to reading their script
some four months later, they called Andrew and Louellen and
said that they already had a similar story "in development"
(which probably meant that they had no such story, but they
might steal this one later and wanted to cover their asses), but
that Andrew and Louellen really had a feel for the characters and
would they like to come in and pitch stories.

Which is where the trouble had really started. Andrew
decided that he and Louellen should see every show *The Plodniks* had ever done in all their three seasons, and he called the
production office surreptitiously to try to get tapes of all the previous shows from one of the underlings there. He talked to a
twenty-one-year-old production assistant named Deena, who
giggled and informed him that the tapes were not allowed to go
off the lot. So Andrew went over to Paramount and flirted with
Deena, who incidentally wasn't bad looking, until she finally

gave him a large stack of videotapes to take home. Something happened the day Andrew returned the tapes, and suddenly he found himself in Deena's shabby postwar apartment—in her bed, no less—on a hot gloomy smoggy afternoon, while Louellen was at work right around the corner. As Andrew drove past Louellen's soundstage on Las Palmas and saw Louellen's bright red Datsun out front, he was disgusted with himself. He hadn't even had enough sense to use a condom! It had been so long since he had slept with anyone besides Louellen that it never even occurred to him that he needed protection until it was too late. Oh, too late! All at once he was certain he was going to die of a terrible disease, all for the sake of forty-five minutes of something like pleasure. In the old days, infidelity was a moral question, punishable by severe feelings of guilt maybe, not death. Andrew went home and took a long shower, scrubbing himself furiously with Louellen's loofah.

When Andrew and Louellen sat in the spacious office of JoAnn and Dan McMann and pitched stories to them and to the other five producers of *The Plodniks of Laguna*, their stories seemed "on the money," but fortunately not too "on the money."

When they ordered lunch, Deena the P.A. brought in all the cartons of food and set them up with plastic silverware on the coffee table. Deena tried not to look at Andrew. She was wearing shorts and white Reeboks with no socks, and her bare ankles were a pleasing yet disturbing sight. Andrew was nervous until she left the room, and then he was still nervous because he couldn't tell whether the producers really liked their stories. At the end of the session JoAnn said that three of their stories might be workable and that she and Dan would go ahead and pitch them to the executive producers within the next couple of weeks and then they'd give Andrew and Louellen a call.

So Andrew thought it was a brilliant idea to invite the McManns to dinner. Which it would have been if the duck hadn't killed JoAnn.

Andrew's dinner was Friday night. This was the menu:

Vermouth Cassis Cocktails

Arugula Salad with Warmed Goat Cheese
and Shallot Vinaigrette

Chiu Chow Braised Duck
Baby Leeks
Steamed Rice

Fresh Lime-Mint Sorbet with
Sliced Mangos

Saturday at five A.M. Andrew and Louellen were roused from sleep by painful stomach cramps and they got in the car and drove to the emergency room at Midway Hospital, where they were given painkillers and sent on their way. The intern said

It must have been the duck.

Five hours later, Dan McMann, hunched over the wheel of his Jaguar, drove JoAnn McMann down the eerie tangled roads of Beachwood Canyon, skirted the ominous hills along Franklin Avenue, and swooped down La Cienega without regard for traffic signals, leaning on his horn to alert the uncaring streets of the urgency of their trip. By the time Dan made the right turn on Beverly Boulevard and the gray glass towers of Cedars–Sinai Medical Center finally came into view, JoAnn had passed out doubled over in the passenger seat. By Saturday afternoon she was pronounced dead.

Certain questions kept colliding in Andrew's head. How was it possible to follow *exactly*, without the slightest deviation, a recipe in the *New York Times Magazine* and kill a person as a result? How? Surely the good folks at the *Times* tested their own concoctions. Although there had been a brief moment as Andrew added the duck to the braising liquid in step 1 when he wondered about the wisdom of introducing a protein into the sauce at that particular juncture. Was it possible that the deadly bacteria had grown in the braising liquid as it sat in the blue-and-white-speckled roasting pan while it cooled completely before going into the refrigerator? Or did something horrible happen to the duck itself as it sat on the countertop unrefrigerated for some eighteen deadly hours? How did ambition lead to inadvertent murder? Were there really any accidents? Maybe not, in which case was it then possible that somehow Andrew had *wanted* to kill JoAnn McMann? No, not possible, he haltingly concluded. He had barely known the woman.

So the real question remained: if Andrew had really wanted to impress this high-powered husband-wife producing team, why did he choose to make Chinese duck? He had never made any kind of duck before, he knew there was a chance (albeit slim) that it could turn out badly, and Chinese was one of the very few national cuisines he knew absolutely nothing about preparing. He could easily have served them something safe and proven: scrumptious grilled fillets of salmon napped with a sauce

of vodka and crème fraîche with fried zucchini blossoms and saffron rice pudding for desert. Or robust osso bucco with sorrel
flan and Andrew's famous porcini risotto. Or veal chartreuse
with enoki tarts and baby root vegetables. Or squid sautéed in its
own ink. All fabulous choices. But no, it had to be duck.

Andrew started cooking on Thursday, the day before they were
to come. He put a four-and-a-half-pound duck in a blue-and-
white-speckled roasting pan with homemade beef stock, soy
sauce, and a cheesecloth bag full of ginger, star anise, orange
peel, garlic, and some hot pepper called *fegara*, which he had to
procure from a Chinese apothecary's shop downtown on Spring
Street. He heated the roasting pan and brought the liquid to
a boil. Then he reduced the heat and simmered for fifteen minutes, at which point, according to instructions, he removed
and discarded the aromatic cheesecloth bag. "Remove and dis-
card?" he said to himself at the time. "So soon?" Removing the
bag would make sense to him if he had intended to store the liquid for an extended period, but he did not, and it seemed to him
a waste; additional aromatic flavors might still be infused into
the braising liquid if he left it in longer. But he told himself that
the *New York Times Magazine* hadn't ever failed him before so
why should it now? And the newness of duck, that flabby white
bird untried in his extensive repertoire, further convinced him
to play by the rules.

At about four-thirty on Friday, Andrew took the duck out of the
refrigerator and cut the fat away from its neck, according to the
recipe. Then, checking frequently from duck to magazine and
back to duck, he placed an empty olive oil bottle in a baking pan

and very carefully lowered the duck onto it, easing the bottle into the duck's neck. It was oddly sexual. Andrew balanced the duck like that and looked at it. Fat was still oozing out of the neck in white curds. It was disgusting. He set it aside.

Louellen came home from work and kissed Andrew behind his ear. She was tall enough to do that easily. How could Andrew have been unfaithful to such a creature? What a stupid, destructive, dangerous thing to do. In Andrew's mind it would have served him right if he had contracted some hideous disease and was doomed. And what if he had already communicated something to Louellen? He could never live with the guilt.

Therefore Andrew decided to go in for testing right away. Monday. Or Tuesday, latest.

Louellen was holding a bunch of big feathery parrot tulips, white and dark red. "Look," she said, holding them up under Andrew's face, "they look exactly like raddichio." And so they did. They must have cost twenty dollars. Louellen had paid for all the groceries for the dinner too. Andrew appreciated and resented Louellen's continual monetary outlay. He was thinking about this while his hands were in the duck. "So you haven't chickened out about making duck," Louellen said, and she started squawking like a laugh. "You're so ambitious, honey!" she said, and as she did, Andrew felt a mild sense of impending doom.

"You set the table," he said, and Louellen put the tulips in a tall vase (and Andrew remembered something that Pilar had taught him long ago: that in Spanish, *tal vez* means "perhaps"). Louellen started ironing the damask tablecloth right onto the table.

Andrew brought the braising liquid to a boil in the roasting pan, removed the duck from its perch on the bottle, and lowered it into the boiling liquid. The juice splashed up onto his purple T-shirt and left a big grease stain. He put cold water on it, but it had no effect on the spot, and now he'd have to find something else to wear. He put a piece of cheesecloth on the duck and it soaked up fat too. As the duck simmered, Andrew basted it now and then. The pan kept filling up with liquefied fat, which Andrew pulled out with the basting bulb. When Louellen saw it she said, "Why waste time? Why don't we just go right ahead and inject some of that directly into our veins?" Andrew had a horrible thought just then. He thought that Deena could have been an intravenous-drug user for all he knew about her. He wouldn't wait until Tuesday; he'd definitely go Monday.

Mango is the fruit that most closely resembles human flesh in consistency. Louellen sat at the kitchen table carving slices off a large mango with a small pointed German knife. The yellow-orange slices fell voluptuously onto the red plate in front of her. She picked up one with her fingers and laid the slice on her tongue. She sat there like that, staring at her busy boyfriend until he finally turned around and looked. When Andrew came over to get it, Louellen swallowed it. "I know about you and the P.A.," she said.

Andrew fell into a chair. He knew he was supposed to feel horrible now, but the truth of the matter was that he felt a great sense of relief.

"I feel so horrible," he said.

"*You* feel horrible?" said Louellen.

"Louellen," he said, and her name sounded weird. Louellen. Louellen Louellen Louellen. He never called her Louellen; he always called her sweetheart or honey or baby. "Baby," he said, "I am so sorry. Of course you know it didn't mean anything."

Louellen just sat there, staring into the tulips. "The thing that astonishes me most," she said finally, "is that you didn't have the good taste to fuck somebody of better breeding."

"The whole thing was a horrible horrible mistake," Andrew said.

"You bet it was," said Louellen. "Perhaps an irreparable mistake."

Tal vez, tal vez.

"I hope you at least had the foresight to protect yourself against disease."

"Of course," said Andrew, really wishing he had. "How did you find out?"

"I saw you starin' at her when we went in there to pitch. I just had a feeling, so I called up and asked the little slut flat out, and threatened to break her jaw if she didn't tell me the truth. Finally she said yes, but that I shouldn't be angry with you—isn't that cute?—because it was she who seduced you."

"That's true . . ."

"I'm not finished. If this ever happens again, you can go ahead and kiss me good-bye, because I assure you I am not a masochist and that will be the end. And don't think you can get away with anything, because you can't. I know you too well. I know everything you're thinking."

Andrew started to say something.

"*And* I know when you've had sex with someone. I can tell by the way your dick feels when it's inside of me."

To Andrew, the enormity of that statement was alarming; and

even if such a thing were impossible, at some level Andrew believed her. "Sweetheart," he said, "do you hate me?"

"Sweetheart," she said, "if I hated you, then I wouldn't care if you slept with some little bimbo." She came over and sat in Andrew's lap and put a slice of mango in his mouth. He put his arms around her, feeling very fortunate, very relieved.

"Just so long as you're sufficiently remorseful," she said. "I mean really dreadfully miserable."

"I am," said Andrew. "I love you so much, baby," he said, kissing Louellen's shoulder.

"Marry me," she said into Andrew's purple cotton chest.

They sat like that for a long time.

Then Andrew knew it was getting late. He kissed Louellen as if to dismiss her and snapped into action. He mixed together the Chinese Chinkiang vinegar with the crushed garlic. It didn't look quite right. He thought if the garlic had been *minced* rather than put through a press, it wouldn't have looked so runny: he could have cut it into neat little square chunks, each with its own integrity. In any case, he poured this slightly imperfect dip into four individual tiny dishes and put them on the table, which Louellen was setting gorgeously. The dark red dishes picked up the red in the tulips, and the black lacquer chopsticks were perfect.

When JoAnn and Dan McMann walked in at eight-fifteen, Andrew was carving the duck. JoAnn poked her head into the kitchen. She was one of those women who doesn't cook. "Something smells marvelous!" she said, and Louellen gave them delightful aperitifs.

The dinner was an enormous success, even though Dan McMann was allergic to Louellen's cat, East L.A., and they had to lock him (the cat, not Dan McMann) in the bedroom for the entire evening, and as it turned out East L.A. took a nap on Dan McMann's jacket, which lay on the bed, and the cat hair made him sneeze all the way home. Also Andrew forgot to change out of his purple T-shirt, and beside the fact that he was under-dressed, there was still an embarrassing grease spot on it. But the duck was delicious, the baby leeks were perfection, mango happened to be JoAnn's absolute favorite fruit. They drank a bottle of 1981 Grgich Hills chardonnay and two bottles of 1982 Acacia St. Claire pinot noir (Andrew felt that the duck was substantial enough to support a pinot but not a cabernet) and they laughed themselves silly. It turned out that Dan and Andrew had both gone to Van Nuys High School, and though Dan was a few years older, they knew many of the same people. By the time the McManns walked out the door just after midnight, Andrew and Louellen were sure they had a sale.

The Loved One

On Monday morning Andrew and Louellen assembled morose clothing for JoAnn McMann's funeral.

Louellen pulled garments out of the closet and threw them on the bed: strapless black cotton sundress, black knit cocktail dress, straight black wool skirt. Though it was February, it was ninety-four degrees outside that day and fires threatened thirty-one homes in Topanga Canyon and Alta Dena. The windows were open in the bedroom, but the air was still and dry. At Forest Lawn Cemetery, in the foothills above Burbank, it would be ten degrees hotter; black wool, though appropriate in mood, would have sizzled on the skin. The air conditioner in Andrew's Honda was out of freon, and Louellen's Datsun was in the shop. Louellen pulled on the skirt anyway, and black hose and a black silk blouse, just to see whether she could stand it. She couldn't. She pulled off her blouse and stood there in the skirt and a black lace bra, peering into the closet the way you might peer into a refrigerator. Her shoulder blades were exquisite.

Andrew found women remarkable. The way they owned and wore lace lingerie, for instance. "Sweetheart," he said. "Why did you buy that bra?"

Louellen turned around, looked blankly at Andrew. "I don't understand the question, darlin'."

"Did you go out and buy it in a department store? Did someone give it to you? Did you buy it for a special purpose? Why does a woman buy a black lace bra?"

"Sweetheart," she said, "I was driving up San Vicente, right by the Beverly Center one day, and this incredible magnetic force pulled my car right up the ramp into the parking lot. Next thing I know I'm in Bullocks department store, in the lingerie department, and this black brassiere is screamin' out at me. The saleslady holds a gun to my head and says, 'Buy it, bitch,' and so you see, I really had no choice in the matter whatsoever." She looked at Andrew as if he were just a little bit crazy, then she put her head back into the closet.

Andrew said, "I mean, did you say to yourself one day, Gee, I really need a black lace bra?"

"You had better think about getting dressed," she said, putting on a smart navy linen suit.

Andrew had nothing to wear. "I can't go," he said. "I have nothing to wear."

"Don't be a silly goose," said Louellen. "Of course you do."

"I'm not a silly goose," he said, getting back into bed. "I'm a silly Andrew." Sometimes he lay there all day when Louellen was at work, but if she had known that, she'd have called him a lazy scumbag. "I can't go to the funeral," he said. "I killed her."

A siren reeled in the distance, maybe flying up Highland

Avenue. Andrew jumped up. "They're coming!" he screamed. "They're coming for me!"

Louellen came over and put her arms around him, kissed his hair, and he calmed down. "Why me?" he said. And then, "I'll never make duck again."

"Of course you will, sweetheart," said Louellen. "Listen," she said then. "You did not kill JoAnn."

"I didn't?" he said. "Then who did?"

"The duck killed her," she said. "The duck killed JoAnn McMann."

These words gave Andrew the strength to dress for the funeral; black slacks materialized, a gray shirt, a somber enough tie. By some miracle Andrew and Louellen made it through the hot drive over the hill on the Hollywood Freeway to the valley side of the hills, made it through the dull service in the airless chapel and the speech by the minister who, though he had never actually met the deceased, knew she was a wonderful person, made it through the monotonous dusty vehicular procession (which was more like a traffic jam) from the chapel to the burial site, made it through the tortuous moment of Dan McMann wailing up to heaven, "Oh, Lord, her time had not yet come!"

After that ordeal, Andrew didn't feel that he had the stamina to make it back over the hill. Louellen couldn't drive a stick shift very well, so rather than destroy his transmission, Andrew suggested they stop at his mother's in the valley on the way home, and take a swim.

Fanny was home. "Hi!" she screamed out the open kitchen window as they walked up the brick path. "My baby!" cried Fanny when they came through the screen door, and she took

Andrew's face in both her hands and kissed him on the cheek.
She looked at him as if he were the most beautiful sight she had
ever seen. "Hello, Louellen," she said then, and Louellen got
kissed too. "Are you devastated?" Fanny said. "Was it horrible?
Do you want some iced tea?"

"I'm parched, Fanny," said Louellen. Andrew had opened
the pantry and was looking for food. "I'd absolutely love some,"
she said.

"We need a gin and tonic," said Andrew.

"Yes," said Fanny. "We do." Louellen still wanted iced tea.

All the doors and windows in the house were open. Fanny
poured Louellen a tall glass of iced tea from a pitcher she took
from the refrigerator. Then she mixed two fairly weak gin and
tonics in the same tall glasses. There was dishwasher scum on the
glasses and there was too much lemon in the iced tea.

"It's sun tea," said Fanny. "I brewed it in the sun."

Andrew found a bathing suit he kept in a drawer in his old
bedroom, and Fanny loaned Louellen a forest green one-piece
with worn-out elastic around the legs. It was about four sizes
too big for her but Fanny couldn't find any of Carmen's. "You
know," she said, "you really ought to keep a suit here."

"Great idea," said Louellen, but that was the last thing she
intended to do. When Louellen came out of the bathroom wearing Fanny's suit, Fanny said, "We could fit a whole extra person
in there with you." Louellen laughed; Andrew decided she must
like his mother. "You've got a gorgeous figure," said Fanny.

The pool was six or seven degrees too warm; Andrew felt
embryonic. Louellen swam lengths at the bottom of the pool,
where it was cooler, pushing off hard from each end, and only
came up at the end of each length, taking deep long breaths.

Andrew watched his mother swim. Though she was overweight, in the pool she was another creature; her strokes were perfect, even, graceful; her head tilted slightly up to the left for each breath; no energy was wasted. The "crawl" did not seem like the proper word to describe so smooth a stroke. This was what Fanny used to call "perfect form."

Louellen bumped Andrew underwater with the top of her head like a shark. When she came sliding up next to him, he had never seen anything so perfectly smooth and cool and delicious as Louellen's wet hairless skin.

So why couldn't Andrew commit to her and break free from the clutches of his mother? The "broken home" theory that Louellen propounded, whereby Andrew had never had positive role models for love relationships since he grew up the product of an unhappy marriage, didn't ring true to him. Fanny and Don always seemed happy until the day Don left. It had always felt to Andrew that he lived in a happy family.

Or had he?

What was happiness, anyway? Lack of argument? His parents had rarely argued, never fought.

Was this normal? Was it even possible? Did they just hide it brilliantly?

Maybe Andrew didn't know how to *feel*. After all, the more he thought about it, the more he understood that Fanny didn't know how to feel. Maybe, after all, that was why Don had left.

Actually, this theory made quite a bit of sense. It would explain why Andrew couldn't seem to feel anything when Louellen confronted him about his idiotic affair. It would explain why he didn't feel any real anger toward Don. And it would also explain why, although he was very full of remorse and considered himself responsible, he didn't really *feel* anything about JoAnn McMann's death.

All at once the matters of duck and death seemed far less important than getting to the bottom of this feeling thing.

This Can't Be Duck

Thursday morning there was a knock on the door and Andrew received a visit from Officer Mattingly of the L.A.P.D., Hollywood precinct. Louellen was in the shower. Andrew invited the officer in.

"I don't want to take up much of your time, Mr. Kelbow," said the officer. "I'd just like to ask you a few questions regarding the death of JoAnn McMann."

This was it. It was happening. It hadn't been a paranoid delusion, Andrew was wanted for murder. He hoped Louellen didn't walk naked into the living room. He'd go in and warn her. But how could he gracefully get out of the room?

"Exactly why did Dan and JoAnn McMann come to your apartment last Friday night?"

"It was sort of business. Sort of social. They came over for dinner."

"I see. And exactly what time did you serve dinner?"

"Oh, gee . . . that's a difficult question. See, I served the first course well before the duck, and it must have been, oh, about . . . nine o'clock."

The interview continued in this vein, until finally the officer revealed that there had been some inconsistencies in Mr. McMann's report, and although he probably shouldn't be saying this, he didn't think that Andrew should worry about his own culpability in the matter.

"What kind of inconsistencies?" said Andrew.

"You stated earlier that you and your, uh, Miss Louellen Berman arrived at Midway Emergency Room at approximately five-twenty A.M.?"

"That's right," said Andrew.

"And that information checks out with Midway."

"Okay . . ."

"Well, it seems Mr. McMann did not check his wife into Cedars-Sinai until shortly after noon. The doctor in charge over there said it's highly unlikely it would take that much longer for the bacteria to affect the McManns. Mr. McMann should not have waited that long to get his wife to the hospital. It seems the McManns have been having marital problems for some time. We suspect foul play."

Louellen came out of the bathroom wrapped in a towel and Officer Mattingly stood up and stared at her for a moment, then quickly turned around.

After he left, Andrew told Louellen that they should go out and celebrate that evening, so she shouldn't hang around with the foley editors after work.

As soon as Louellen was out the door, Andrew picked up the phone and called Fanny. "Mom, your son's a free man," he told her, and she said, "Oh, yay!"

"I didn't kill JoAnn McMann after all—her husband did. She could have been saved."

Later, when he went out to get the mail, there was an envelope from Blue Cross. It was about a health-insurance claim from when he'd had appendicitis the year before; included was a check for fifteen hundred dollars. This was astonishing, because Blue Cross had already reimbursed his doctor! It was a mistake! "It never rains," he said, picking up East L.A. and kissing the top of his head. Of course he'd keep the money; God knew he paid enough in inflated coverage rates over the past year.

That night he wouldn't tell Louellen where they were having dinner, and she kept trying to guess as they drove east across Hollywood.

Musso & Frank?

she said. "Nope," said Andrew. "Guess again."

Katsu?

"Gezundheit," he said. "Guess again."

The Pantry?
Mon Kee?
Pacific Dining Car?
Le Petit Chaya?

she said, incredulous. There weren't too many restaurants east of Cahuenga in those days. Except for Thai places. "I know," she said. "Chao Praya."

"Wrong again," said Andrew. He took a right on Hollywood Boulevard, crossed Edgemont, crossed Vermont. He made a right turn into a long, fairly empty parking lot. Set way back from the street, there it was. The imperial archway of the Shanghai.

Andrew hadn't been there since his ninth birthday. The paint wasn't peeling yet, but it was a little duller, a little shabbier than he remembered. The waiters looked older; perhaps they were the same ones who had always worked there. The menu said

Our Specialty
PEKING DUCK
Please Order 24 Hours in Advance

Andrew panicked for a moment; without Peking duck the event would have no meaning. Then he motioned the waiter over. The tall, stern Chinese man came over to the table, leaned forward slightly. Did Andrew remember him from his childhood? Andrew pressed a bill into his hand. "We have a yen for Peking duck," he said. "We didn't think about calling ahead."

The waiter nodded solemnly. "No problem, kid," he said, walking slowly away.

"How much did you give him?" said Louellen.

Andrew said, "Don't worry your pretty little head about it." He had given him a five. Bribes are incredibly affordable in less-than-fashionable circles.

The platter came at last. The pancakes. The scallions. The ritual. The duck was heaven. Louellen adored it too. It was the happiest Andrew had felt in years.

A Brief History of
Botulism in America

In 1963, the fact that fourteen Americans died during the year in two botulism epidemics hadn't escaped Fanny. Smoked fish was the culprit in a number of the cases, canned tuna in the rest. Canned tuna's involvement was something that was so upsetting to Fanny that she couldn't really let herself think about it as much as she might have. Instead, she busied herself worrying about broken glass in cans, and checking carefully when she removed the lids with her electric can opener (which always had an oily brown crust on the blade that she couldn't completely remove, and smelled vaguely of chocolate malteds, for some unexplained reason), and her beloved Bumble Bee brand had never been tainted by botulism anyhow.

In April 1970, eighty thousand frozen pizzas garnished with botulistic mushrooms made their way onto grocery shelves. No problem for the Kelbows, because Fanny wouldn't touch a frozen pizza with a ten-foot spatula. And just to be safe, she scrupulously avoided all mushrooms save fresh ones.

But the next year a banker and his wife sat down to dinner at their home in Bedford Village, New York. The wife had opened a can of Bon Vivant brand vichyssoise, which she cleverly pretended to have made herself. She poured it into bowls, garnished it with a dainty sprinkling of chopped chives, and the couple sipped it contentedly, alternating between bites of Sara Lee Parker House rolls, before moving on to their next course. The next morning, the banker suffered double vision as he tried to button his vest, and when he tried to mention this to his wife, he had trouble speaking. When suddenly he couldn't move his arms and legs, his wife rushed him to the hospital but alas, too late. The botulism killed him. His wife, whose digestive system had always moved just a tad slower than her dearly departed husband's, became gravely ill, but eventually she recovered, and survived.

Fanny read all about it in the paper. *Bacterium Clostridium botulinum* the toxin was called. "A few ounces of it," the newspaper reported a top scientist as saying, "could kill all human beings on earth." Harmful effects, she read, usually show up between eighteen and ninety-six hours after eating, and usually cause a paralysis of the respiratory system or heart failure.

Lo these many years later, when JoAnn McMann died of it after eating at Andrew's house, Fanny remembered the *between eighteen and ninety-six hours* part. This was what didn't make sense to her.

"That's what doesn't make sense to me," she had said to Andrew, after he came back from the hospital. "You guys got sick eleven, twelve, one, two, three, four, five . . . that's seven hours after you ate the duck."

"That's right," said Andrew. "The reason it doesn't make sense to you is that it wasn't botulism. It was just food poisoning—probably campylobacter if it made her that sick."

"Oh," said Fanny. "I've been telling everyone it was botulism."

"Of course you have," said Andrew. "Botulism is so much more romantic."

"Anyway," said Fanny, "thank God *that's* over."

What Happens When You Assume

It was a foregone conclusion that Little Mike and Carmen would indeed get married, but no one thought it would happen so soon. Fanny and Edward told them they were too young to get married, but when did that ever stop anybody?

Fanny didn't know exactly why it was important to Little Mike to marry so young. He was only twenty-one, even younger than Fanny when she married Don. And what a mistake *that* had been.

This is what it was: he had been waiting for twenty-one years to achieve something that Andrew hadn't yet achieved in his lifetime of overachievement. It was within his grasp, and he'd be a fool not to grab it.

This is why Little Mike had announced his engagement to Carmen last time Andrew brought Louellen to dinner at Fanny's—it was apparent that Andrew was serious enough about her to be considering marriage himself, and Little Mike couldn't afford to take any chances of missing his only opportunity.

And so the night Little Mike announced his engagement to Carmen was also the night Carmen learned of it herself. The rest of the family assumed that it had been discussed at length already and mutually agreed upon by the two young lovers; no one imagined that even Little Mike would dare make such a bold pronouncement without being sure of the outcome.

But lack of self-confidence was never Little Mike's affliction. To Little Mike, Carmen's acceptance was so certain that rejection seemed impossible. As indeed it probably was: Carmen wanted to be with Little Mike forever, she knew that, and so she found nothing wrong with his unusual method of proposal. It was too early and she was too young still to foresee that the cocky announcement would set a tone that would be dangerous for the future of their marriage; instead she perceived his willfulness as manly-cute.

There was the question of who would pay for the wedding. It was so obvious that Carmen couldn't count on her mother to contribute that she didn't even bother to ask her; in fact, she didn't tell her she was engaged until the day she needed help addressing the envelopes for the invitations. It wasn't only that Carmen's mother didn't have any money to help, but also that she was so utterly embittered against men that she had not even dated one since her own husband, Carmen's father, had walked out on her eleven years earlier, and she didn't trust Little Mike any more than she trusted Carmen's father.

"Doesn't she know that it's extremely bad luck not to give your daughter your blessing when she gets married?" said Fanny.

Carmen said, "I guess they didn't think so in Mexico."

~~~

In the past, Carmen had been quite close to her father, a well-to-do film director who lived in Malibu. But he had remarried three years ago, and his young and beautiful wife had recently given birth to a baby girl who was suddenly all Carmen's father could think about. Now it took a week before he would even get around to returning Carmen's call. To compensate for the lack of time he was spending with her, he had begun making promises to Carmen, promises of more time together after his next picture, promises of vacations with his wife and the new baby (which didn't sound even vaguely appealing to Carmen), promises that finally degenerated into the realms of money and of merchandise.

For Carmen's twenty-first birthday her father gave her a gift certificate from Neiman-Marcus.

He even promised her his car, a white 1984 BMW 320i, as soon as he took delivery of his new Jaguar, which didn't come and didn't come and didn't come. When Carmen's 1962 Volkswagen bug coughed and sputtered and choked and died an undistinguished death trying to make it over the Sepulveda Pass in the slow lane, she sat in the hot car on the shoulder of the San Diego Freeway in the shadow of a dry yellow mountain and put her forehead on the steering wheel and cried.

Carmen's father was the type of successful director who went from picture to picture without too many periods of unemployment, but he lived so lavishly, especially since he'd married the young beauty, that he could never seem to earn enough to catch up with his spending. So all he could offer Carmen for her wedding was the use of his beach house at Malibu and ten cases of champagne.

Little Mike knew that the reason he offered them the beach house was so that his friends and all the important show-biz connections whom he insisted on inviting would think that he was paying for the wedding. Of course Little Mike didn't dare say this to Carmen, who steadfastly refused to admit to anyone, even her fiancé, that her father had any flaws at all.

Carmen wanted to have seventy-five people at an informal reception, and she became wretched because she had no idea how she could swing it.

Edward grabbed Fanny one evening after dinner. "Fanny," he said. "We can pay for it."

"We can?" said Fanny. "No, we can't. We can't afford it. Are you sure?"

"Let's do it," said Edward. "I feel like she's our own daughter already anyway."

If you think about it, Edward never did have any children of his own.

It was one of the best moments of Fanny's life; if she ever doubted it before, she knew in that instant that she had married the greatest man in the world.

"We'll make Don pay for the rehearsal dinner," Edward said.

"Yeah," said Fanny. "And let's tell Carmen and Little Mike to have it someplace real fabulous and expensive so he really gets stuck."

That night Fanny told Little Mike the good news. "Edward's going to pay for your wedding," she said. "Can you believe how nice he is?"

"You mean *you* and Edward are going to pay for our wedding," he said.

"Right," said Fanny. "You don't seem very pleased."

"I am," he said. "It's really great of you guys. You're the best." He kissed Fanny's cheek.

Fanny wasn't sure why she was so angry.

"It was Edward's idea, you know. I think it's really generous of him," she said.

"Of course it is," said Little Mike. "It's wonderful. We'd probably have to elope otherwise."

"So what are you so pissed off for?" said Fanny.

"I'm not pissed off, crazy. But I just think you shouldn't think of it as *Edward's* money. Even though he makes most of it. Haven't you ever heard of community property?"

"That's not the point," said Fanny. "You guys just never give Edward any credit."

"No," said Little Mike. "That's not the point. *You* never give *yourself* any credit. That's the point."

The whole thing upset Fanny so much that she couldn't sleep at all that night, and when she got out of bed in the middle of the long night to pee, Otto took her spot under the covers, and she couldn't move him at all, not an inch, and his heavy head was on her pillow, as if *he* were Edward's wife, and Edward was snoring, loudly, so finally there was nothing else to do but make herself a baloney sandwich and sit up in the living room and read and watch it getting light outside.

The next day was somewhat better. Don agreed without argument when Little Mike asked him to pay for dinner for thirty-five at the Bistro Garden in Beverly Hills; he had no suspicions whatsoever of the scheme that had been perpetrated against him, thinking instead that he was simply doing something nice, if extravagant, to honor his son and his son's betrothed. It made him feel old.

Little Mike asked Andrew to be his best man.

Andrew, for his part, understood that the time had come to make some decisions about his own life. It wasn't fair to Louellen to keep her hanging like this. He felt vaguely restless, wholly unsatisfied—not with Louellen so much as with his whole life.

He resolved to . . . resolve.

Correction

CORRECTION: Because of editing errors, the recipe for Chiu Chow braised duck in the Jan. 25 Food column is wrong in part. The duck should not be added to the braising liquid until step three, the garlic in step four should be minced, and the cheesecloth bag of spices should not be removed unless the liquid is to be stored for an extended period.

—*The New York Times Magazine*
February 15, 1987

The Consultation

Pilar showed up in Edward's office one day for a consultation. She was wearing a simple blue cotton dress and a string of pearls—Edward had never seen her in anything but work clothes, usually black. He took the fact that she was chewing on her pearls to mean that she was nervous.

"Please sit down, Pilar," he said. "Make yourself comfortable, relax."

Pilar looked around at the opulent surroundings. The Persian rugs that covered almost every square inch of the oiled wood floors were all gifts from Iranian clients, and there were beautiful Oriental porcelain pieces in antique mahogany display cases, all thank-you gifts as well.

Pilar looked up at Edward. "I want a green card," she said.

"Fine," said Edward. "But let me explain a few things to you."

Pilar sat in front of him expectantly, her hands folded in her lap now.

232 ♦ LESLIE BRENNER

Edward sat back in his enormous chair. "You're retired, Pilar," he said. "Has Ken also retired?"

"He still owns the landscaping service," said Pilar.

"Fine," he said. "Pilar, I'm going to be honest with you. You don't really need a green card. You're not working, and the chances of anyone ever asking Ken whether he has one are slim to none at this point in his career. Just out of curiosity, why do you want to go through this after all these years?"

"I want to become a citizen of the U.S.A.," she said. "I want to be an American."

"You *are* an American, Pilar," said Edward. "How long have you been here—thirty years?"

"Thirty-two," she said. "I want an American passport. I want to travel to Europe someday, and maybe to Japan. And someday to visit Mexico again."

"Okay," said Edward. "I understand." He explained to her that the following year there would be a national amnesty program for aliens, and she and Ken would have no problem qualifying since they had been continuously in the country for so long. "So therefore," he said, "I could do the work for you now, but it would be rather complicated and expensive. Of course I'd give you a greatly reduced hourly fee. But what I suggest is that since your case is not urgent, you should wait until after January first of next year, and then we'll apply for amnesty under the new law. I would be happy to handle the case for you at that time free of charge."

"Okay," said Pilar. "Thank you." She looked as if she might cry.

"Do you understand, Pilar? Is that what you would like to do?"

"Yes," said Pilar. "That would be good." She stood up.

"Are you okay?" said Edward.

"Yes," she said. "I'm just so happy."

When Edward showed her to the door, she hugged him.

Oh, that's swell," said Fanny when Edward told her about the meeting later that evening. "We'll have to invite her to the wedding."

"Absolutely," said Little Mike. "I couldn't get married without Pilar there."

"You grew up with her," said Fanny. "She changed your diapers."

"That's right," said Little Mike, and he looked thoughtful. "She was like a cleaning lady to me."

Everybody Fanny Knew

Everybody Fanny knew was in Carmen's father's backyard, plus a lot of people she didn't know.

It was a hot day in August, even at the beach, and there was a forest fire out in Thousand Oaks that reddened the horizon and blew ashes into the sky all over Los Angeles.

The wedding was a great success; the ceremony was short and simple and Fanny's mother Rose was thrilled that it had been performed by a rabbi. Carmen and Little Mike had done just about everything themselves. The only glitch was that Little Mike was wearing a morning suit that didn't fit him properly; the pants legs were two or three inches too long and they bagged up around his new black shoes.

"Fanny," said Priscilla, walking up to her with a smirk on her face and an invitation in her hand, "they ended the wedding invitation in a preposition." She was right, unfortunately, for Carmen had designed and written the invitations herself. They said:

The ceremony will be
followed by a reception at
2324 Malibu Colony Road,
which we hope you will come to.

"I'm surprised you didn't catch the dangling modifier," said Fanny, "a much more egregious error. The good news is nothing's misspelled."

Edward was standing a little hunched over, with his arm around Rose, who had tears in her eyes from the moment she boarded the plane in Newark.

"Just—bee-yoo-tee-ful!" Rose kept saying, and even though she thought they were too young to get married, she much preferred it to the previous arrangement of the two living together, unwed, with Fanny and Edward. As for her feelings about Edward, she had been suspicious of him when she first met him, but as soon as he married Fanny, she embraced him as a son.

"Carmen looks absolutely—bee-yoo-tee-ful!" Rose said to Fanny.

"If you don't look good in a wedding dress, you've got a big problem," said Fanny.

But Rose never forgave Don for leaving Fanny, and she never forgave Fanny for letting him go, although she was finally beginning to accept the fact that Fanny was much happier with Edward in the long run than she ever could have been with Don. All Rose could think about during the five-hour plane trip was how she dreaded seeing Don, whom she adored and detested so much. Last night at the rehearsal dinner, she saw him for the first time in years. She was shaking like a leaf when they embraced, and Don thought it was simply the effects of old age, but Rose knew that even though she was eighty-two years old, it wasn't age that made her shake.

Don and Valentina posed for a picture with Carmen and Little Mike and Andrew. Don was beaming so hard that Little Mike thought his face would break. Little Mike was annoyed at Don's extreme pride on his wedding day; after all, Don had not exactly raised him from a pup. On the other hand, there was no one in the world who meant as much to him as Andrew, his best man, his brother.

When the picture broke up, Louellen kissed Carmen's cheek. "I am so happy for you," she said. "And you are truly a lovely bride."

"Oh, thank you," said Carmen. "And I know you'll be a lovely bride too."

"Yes, indeed," said Louellen. "If I ever *do* become a bride. I may remain a spinster for the rest of my life if Andrew doesn't get on the stick, so to speak."

Don took Little Mike and Carmen aside. He was still beaming aggressively.

"Does your face hurt?" said Little Mike, and Don laughed.

"I want to tell you about your wedding present now," said Don, and he suddenly became very serious. He looked at each of them in turn. "I'm buying you a place setting."

Carmen looked at Don and wondered if he could possibly be serious.

"No, seriously," he said. "I'm sending you to Hawaii for two weeks for a honeymoon."

The newlyweds were thrilled, because otherwise they wouldn't have had a honeymoon, and they both kissed Don and thanked him profusely. And then Little Mike began to feel guilty for thinking bad thoughts about his father just a moment before.

"We'll see if he comes through," said Fanny when Carmen told her about Don's present; then suddenly Carmen started.

"What is it?" said Fanny.

"The flowers," she said. "Look at the flowers."

On each of the small rented tables around the patio there was an arrangement of red roses and white carnations.

"I didn't order red and white," said Carmen. "I ordered yellow and white."

"Oh, my God," said Fanny. "They're bad luck. The florist screwed up."

Carmen gazed at them for a while. Her father and his wife and the baby were sitting at one of the tables. The baby poured a glass of champagne on her father's head, and they all laughed. "Oh, well," said Carmen at last. "It doesn't mean anything. It's just a silly superstition."

"That's right," said Fanny. "It's stupid."

So Little Mike and Carmen were married. "Carmen Kelbow," people were saying, and it did have a certain ring to it.

As the afternoon wore on, the sun became hotter, and by five o'clock there were ashes from the forest fire in everyone's champagne.

Doggy Heaven

Edward had always hated living in the house in Van Nuys. He never got over the feeling that it was really Don's house, even after he jettisoned the green thing; there remained forever a kind of Don-presence there in spite of all Edward's renovations.

The house reminded Edward constantly of Fanny's past with Don, and this was something Edward didn't feel he should have to think about any longer.

Besides that, the valley oppressed him. He had moved there from Brooklyn in 1958, but in those days the valley was gorgeous: the orange groves were insane with fruit, and smog, when it did appear, was confined to the farthest reaches of Burbank and the East Valley. But by 1987 the orange groves were all but gone, traffic was a nightmare, and Van Nuys Boulevard had lost what little charm it once had. The sky was uniformly brown, and it sat over the valley like a veil of steel wool. Once or twice or maybe three times a year, in the fall, the Santa Ana wind would come in, malevolent and hot as a Korean gardener's leaf blower, and send the smog west to the Pacific Ocean. But after a day or two of clear, still heat, the smog would return again and sit there as if it had never been disturbed.

Since Little Mike and Carmen would soon be moving out into their own apartment, Edward wanted to move to the hills, to a new house.

"I don't want to," said Fanny. "I've lived here for a hundred years."

And Edward wouldn't settle for the valley side of the hills either; he wanted greenery, fresh air, cool breezes; he wanted to live in Brentwood or Bel-Air or Santa Monica Canyon—someplace fitting for one of the most successful immigration lawyers in Los Angeles. Someplace where Otto might run with the coyotes.

"But I love this house," said Fanny.

"You hate this house," said Edward.

"Oh," said Fanny. "I see."

"This house stinks," said Edward. "You complain about it constantly."

"I complain about Little Mike constantly, and I love him."

"That's different," said Edward.

"No," said Fanny. "It's exactly the same. I want to stay here and watch Iran-contra on C-Span."

Edward pried Fanny's fingers off of the doorjamb and dragged her with him to look at houses.

The first house was in Pacific Palisades.

"Reagan country," said Fanny as Edward negotiated the curves of Sunset Boulevard.

"Fanny," said Edward. "Please reserve judgment until you at least see it."

The real estate agent who met them there was overwhelmingly annoying. The house had a gorgeous canyon view but no pool.

"I love it," said Fanny. "Let's buy it."

"Don't be silly, Fanny," said Edward. "We need a pool."

Fanny said they could put one in.

"Besides," said Edward under his breath. "They're asking seven hundred thousand dollars."

"For this dump?" she said.

"Let's keep looking," said Edward. "There's tons of stuff out there."

Fanny was exhausted after the third house. "This is terrible," she said. "We'll never find a house."

"Of course we will," he said.

"Why don't we just move in with Andrew and Louellen."

After that, Fanny started liking every house they saw and Edward found something wrong with all of them.

Three weeks later, in Mandeville Canyon, they found one.

"I love it," said Fanny. "It's so close to Gelson's." (There was a Gelson's in nearby Pacific Palisades, as well as the two in the valley and one in Century City. If she lived near enough to a Gelson's, her daily life couldn't change that drastically.) And not only was there a pool lined with beautiful Mexican tiles, but there was a redwood deck overlooking a wilderness of canyon, and no other houses in sight.

"Otto will love it," said Edward. "He'll think he died and went to doggy heaven."

That Oedipal Thing

When the time came to move, Fanny asked Andrew to help her pack boxes. He and Louellen were supposed to go to Palm Springs that weekend, but Fanny asked him to postpone the trip because she was worried that she couldn't get everything packed up in time for the movers to come. Little Mike and Carmen obviously couldn't help because they were in Hawaii on their honeymoon.

Louellen was furious. "You'd do anything she asked you," she accused.

"What's wrong with that?" said Andrew. "She's my mother."

"Well, now, if *that* isn't the understatement of the century."

"Sweetheart," said Andrew, "this is traumatic for her. She's lived in that house for over twenty years."

"Big deal," said Louellen. "I've been planning this trip for over twenty minutes."

Louellen won. Andrew went to Palm Springs with her,

LESLIE BRENNERLESLIE BRENNER

although he felt so guilty the whole time he couldn't relax, and he hated the desert and he hated the sun, and when he returned, he helped his mother pack boxes every single day for the next three weeks.

The Conversation with
the Flying Plates

When Andrew was in the attic helping Fanny pack, he found a piece of china that made him shiver. It was a plain, thin, white china plate, inscrutable as the moon. He stared at the plate, not quite recognizing it, but somehow it was familiar. It seemed vaguely dangerous.

Then he knew. He remembered something he had not thought about once since it had happened.

He was nine years old and Fanny was screaming at Don. She was shrieking. Andrew had never heard his mother shriek like this before. Fanny was in the kitchen; she was unloading the dishwasher.

Andrew saw this all suddenly, seventeen years later, with shocking clarity.

The glasses sparkled as Fanny put them in the cupboard. The shelf paper was plaid, white and avocado green. Fanny was wearing a mauve blouse with leaf-shaped swirls on it. Don was sitting at the dining room table. He stood up when Fanny started shrieking. Fanny yelled louder as she slammed the cupboard closed and rolled out the bottom dishwasher rack. "Why don't you say something?" she screamed at Don, but Andrew remembered wondering how his father could possibly say anything with Fanny screaming like that. And then his mother was throwing the dishes, flinging them like Frisbees, aiming them at Don's head, and Don ducked as each dish whizzed past him and smashed against the dining room wall. And then Andrew remembered what Fanny was screaming. She was screaming, "How could you do it, how could you fuck your secretary all of a sudden after twelve years of marriage, how could you do it you bastard, it's such a fucking cliché."

It was the only time Andrew ever heard his parents fight.

Andrew wiped the dust off the plate with his T-shirt. Then he held it up and looked for his reflection, which either wasn't there or else he couldn't see it.

"What are you doing?" said Fanny.

Andrew was quiet for a moment.

"Is this the only one of these plates you have?" he said at last.

"They all broke," said Fanny. "Just put it in that 'miscellaneous kitchen' box."

Andrew stared at the plate. He held it in his hand. Then he curled his arm toward his body and flung the plate with all of his strength, Frisbee-style, at the beamed wall of the attic, and the plate hit the beams and shattered into a million pieces. It didn't feel as good as it should have. Still, it was cathartic. He wished he had more to smash.

Fanny walked over to the wall and picked up one of the shards. "Wrap up this one piece and pack it away," she said.

The Road to Hell

That wasn't the only thing that Andrew remembered as he helped Fanny move out of the house of his childhood; smashing the china plate unleashed a whole string of remembrances.

He remembered that on the night after they moved to Van Nuys they had eaten dinner at Hamburger Hamlet on Van Nuys Boulevard and he had eaten a bowl of lobster bisque and thrown up as soon as they got to the new house.

He remembered one time when Fanny made them all hide in the closet because her sister-in-law dropped in to visit, and when she walked up the brick path and rang the doorbell, none of them answered. Later Fanny swore him and Little Mike to secrecy, making them promise not to tell Don they hid from his brother's redheaded, pinch-nosed wife.

He remembered The Quiet Time, which he had completely forgotten.

And he remembered a scene between his mother and Don,

sometime after Don had left, in which Don returned, presumably for a trial reconciliation.

They were all sitting in the den, watching TV, Andrew, Fanny, and Little Mike; he remembered they were watching *Get Smart*. Peanuts started barking because a car had pulled into the driveway, and when they looked out the window they saw that it was his father's Mercedes. "Stay here," said Fanny, and Andrew and Little Mike continued to look out the window, which afforded a view of the front door, partially obscured by a Chinese elm.

Don was carrying a suitcase.

"Hi," said Fanny. "Did you break up with her?"

"Not yet," said Don, as he reached the threshold. "But I'm going to."

The scene ended there, and Andrew and Little Mike knew, even at the time, never to mention it.

Wanderlust

Fanny threw up the day the movers came. It was the first time she had thrown up in twenty-three years; it left in her mouth a taste like sawdust.

The movers were brutal, flinging boxes that were not particularly well packed anyway. "Okay," said Fanny, toughening; the morning was the culmination of something, an ordeal. "You can smash the china that has been in my family for generations, but you can never take *this* away from me." (She was clinging desperately to the newel post that five years earlier Edward had coated with Zip Strip and watched the old white paint bubble up under the acidic slime—all this an effort to rid the permanent fixtures of the house of any lingering Don-ness.) Fanny felt the grain of the bare post; the movers walked around her through the door with boxes.

"There goes my life," she said to Otto.

"What is it, Fanny?" said Edward, coming through with directions for the movers.

"Let's not move," said Fanny.

"Oh, Fanny," he said. "You're being silly. You'll love the new house."

Fanny looked down at Otto. "Am I being silly?" she said to the dog.

They were ready to go. The fragile pieces were in the BMW, which Edward would drive, and Otto would go in the Volvo with Fanny.

Otto sat in the passenger seat, looking out the window like a person.

Edward started his car and turned to check on Fanny's progress. She walked over to his window. "Go ahead," she said. "I'll just be a minute."

"Are you sure?" said Edward.

"Go ahead," she said.

Edward drove off without looking back.

Fanny sat on the low brick steps of the porch. It was September and the leaves of the sprawling black walnut tree were bright yellow, beginning to fall. The walnuts, black in their oily husks, would be ripe. Fanny had lived in this house for twenty-three years and suddenly she was sorry she had never once climbed the walnut tree.

Sigh of Relief

The day Andrew finished helping Fanny pack up the house in the valley was the same day Louellen started packing Andrew's belongings.

"What's this?" he said, when he came home to find his utensils in a box and Louellen in a snit.

"You're moving out, and we're breaking up," said Louellen, waving a potato masher in the air in the manner of a mad conductor. "I'm fed up." Louellen didn't worry about where Andrew would stay: she knew he would go to Fanny's.

Fanny, upon learning the news, breathed a sigh of relief. For his part, Andrew was partially relieved, and partially chagrined that he wasn't the one to take matters in hand. First, it wasn't fair to make Louellen do it. And second, he was finally feeling resolved that they should part.

So why the hesitation? He didn't exactly know what to do.

As much as Andrew loved motion pictures, he had come to hate show business. In the beginning he could jump into schmooze-mode on command with great and glorious Hollywood zeal, for these were the Dom Pérignon days of the development deal, and he who schmoozed best finished first. But as time wore on, instances like the time he and Louellen had gone in to pitch in the 9200 Sunset building, in the office of the man who had run Twentieth Century–Fox just five years before, occurred with more frequency. Sitting across the desk (which the former studio head looked to be holding down with his feet, as if now that he no longer had a major studio to run, he should play up the cliché mogul image) from the balding, cigar-smoking producer, Andrew and Louellen pitched, in rapid succession, their three best feature ideas, saving, of course, the best for last; this best, however, met with the same dull look on the face of the producer as the first two. The depressing part was they only got a chance to do the one-line pitches. The way this was done was that you first told the story in one line, and since this was the latter half of the 1980s, it had damn well better be "high-concept." If the producer liked the one-line, you could go on to the three-minute pitch, and if that went well, you were on your way to a development deal.

Having spent their three best ideas, alternating Louellen–Andrew–Louellen, Andrew decided to utilize their special "car idea" tactic.

"Is that all you got?" the producer said, starting to remove his feet from the desk so he could show them out.

"Well, actually," said Andrew, calculatedly hesitant. "We did have sort of the germ of a wild idea in the car on the way over here." The truth was, they had thought of it a few days before, and it was *so* stupid, someone might actually go for it.

The mogul's feet went back on the desk, as he braced himself for the one-line.

"*Blood Cruise*," said Andrew, and he could see the mogul brighten a little. "A bunch of wild cats get loose from the cargo hold of a cruise ship and wreak havoc on the first-class passengers."

The mogul puffed thoughtfully on his cigar. "Lions or tigers?" he finally asked.

"Panthers," said Andrew, leaning forward conspiratorially.

"I love it," said the mogul.

They wound up having a three-hour lunch with the guy, who, over espresso, asked them to write a "quick" forty-page treatment. After two weeks of work, and half a dozen arguments about whether the cats should be lions after all or the original panthers or a variety-pak assortment, and whether it should be a huge cruise liner or a smaller, more exclusive vessel, they finally turned it in. They waited a week, and never heard back. They called the guy, but he wouldn't return their calls.

This, then, was Hollywood; and it wouldn't have been so bad if they didn't have to endure the parties. And this was Andrew's life: all the more horrible, because he felt he had been promised so much. He had the best education, he worked his ass off, he schmoozed tirelessly—what was wrong? He hated where he was and what he was doing. Not only that, but his unemployment insurance was about to run out, and the thought of having to find freelance video-editing work or, horror of horrors, signing on with a temp agency to do word processing long enough to qualify for unemployment again made him want to vomit. Suddenly, and this was unusual, he felt like seeing his dad, who, for all his faults, did seem to have a healthy perspective on show business. But more than that, he needed to gather strength, he needed to reconnoiter. No, then, it wouldn't be Don's—what better place than Fanny's?

West Is the Best

Fanny and Edward Alter moved to the Westside in 1987, along with a large percentage of the nation's homeless, who, looking for warmth, went as far west as they could possibly go.

The homeless slept in the doorways of deserted shops along Wilshire Boulevard in Santa Monica, they slept in Dumpsters in the alleys behind McDonald's and The Ivy at the Shore and the thriving businesses of the new mall, they slept under the pier on the wet sand and in shantytowns on Venice Beach.

Fanny made it a habit to walk for at least an hour a day on her days off, and one of her favorite walks was along the palisade park, just across Ocean Avenue from Don and Valentina's new condominium. Sometimes she convinced Andrew to walk with her, even at the risk of angering him by knocking on his door when he was working on his screenplay; it was worth it on the off chance that they'd be able to walk together along the lovely palm-lined grassy strip overlooking the wide stretch of sand of Santa Monica Beach and the Pacific Ocean that was a gorgeous blue until you got up close to it. Andrew wasn't always in a great mood these days, but Fanny was ecstatic that he had come to stay with them, albeit temporarily. They could see the Santa Monica pier down below, and that was their goal. Half of it had been washed away several years before in the apocalyptic rainstorms that destroyed the homes of the very rich in Malibu.

Homeless people had gathered at the north end of the park, which is where Fanny and Andrew began their walk, near where San Vicente meets Ocean Avenue. The homeless sat at the redwood picnic tables near the barbecues, and there was always something smoldering in those pits, though it didn't smell like any food that Fanny or Andrew could recognize. The way they gathered there looked conspiratorial, impenetrable, and dark, and it frightened Fanny.

This long strip of park was one of the few places where people walked in Los Angeles, and they walked for the sake of walking. Ocean Avenue was lined with retirement homes, and the old people came and sat in the park on folding chairs with fat strips of blue and green webbing; they sat under umbrellas and played cards, or conversed, or else they just looked out over the beach to the water. Young lawyers and writers and rich women came out of the expensive condominiums in their sweats and jogged along the dirt path next to the avenue, or walked briskly along the precipice, passing Iranian families—they always called themselves Persians—who ambled along. The high palisades were built on sand, though, and there were signs of erosion everywhere and small placards warning the public to

USE PARK AT YOUR OWN RISK.

When Fanny came for her walk, she always brought some left-over food to give to the homeless, whether it was the remains of some fabulous meal they had had in a restaurant, or something she had made herself. But she was afraid of the homeless and she would only hand the bag of food to a single homeless person in the south end of the park: they were scarier in the north end, the way they always converged in a group. She found it difficult to make eye contact, but she always made some comment or joke about the quality of the food inside the doggy bag.

On their way back from the pier, Fanny thought about the oxidation of fat cells and stepped up the pace. "I love living here," she said. "Look how gorgeous it is." It was a warm, clear, windy day, bright blue sky, a few puffy white clouds. They stopped at the rail and looked out over the water. The usually flat Santa Monica Bay was tipped with whitecaps; sailboats were out despite the fact that it was already November, and Fanny and Andrew could see all the way to Catalina Island.

Later, as they walked on toward the car, Andrew noticed a guy lying on his bundle of clothes on the grass, masturbating in the skinny shade of a palm tree. He stepped in front of Fanny so she wouldn't have to look at it. He turned around, and he didn't see Fanny for a moment, and then he saw that she was standing ten yards back talking to someone.

It was Don.

"Hi, Dad," said Andrew when he came back to them. Don's building was right across the street, and he had been standing at the rail, looking at the ocean—his idea of exercise.

"I come here every day," Fanny was saying to her ex-husband. "I love it here. Why didn't you tell me the Westside was so great?"

"You didn't ask," said Don, and they all laughed and looked out at Catalina.

"How are you feeling?" said Fanny, and Don said that he was much better. "The sea air is very healing," he said.

"Negative ions," said Fanny. "Right? I read that somewhere."

Don squinted. "Something like that," he said. "Hey, I hear your new house is wonderful. You'll have to invite me over sometime."

"You're invited," said Fanny. "It's beautiful; we love it. We've had seven deer and two rattlesnakes. You can see the ocean from the backyard."

Andrew stood there, watching his parents, who were somehow like strangers with each other, and at the same time not.

Thursday was Andrew's birthday, and Fanny and Edward were taking him to dinner, along with Carmen and Little Mike, to celebrate.

"Oh, by the way," said Don. "When would you like to come over for a birthday dinner?"

"I don't know," said Andrew. "Sunday?"

"I'll check with Valentina," said Don.

A few minutes later, when Andrew and Fanny reached the car, Fanny said, "Isn't that just like Don not to think of your birthday until three days before?"

"If Don wasn't Don," said Andrew, "he wouldn't be Don."

Bushed

Shortly after Fanny and Edward had moved into the Mandeville Canyon house, Andrew moved in with them, occupying the large bedroom in the back of the house, with a view of the pool and the canyon. He needed to regroup. He wanted to use the time to work on his screenplay, but, predictably, he was blocked.

By the end of 1987 it was already painfully clear that George Bush would be the Republican nominee for president, and when the Democratic Party nominated Michael Dukakis in June 1988, Andrew decided he would do his part and work on the Dukakis campaign. "If I can convince just *one* person not to vote for Bush, I'll be happy," he said, and drove down the hill and wound along Sunset Boulevard toward the ocean to the out-of-business savings and loan in Pacific Palisades where Democratic headquarters had set up shop. "I'm here to offer my services," Andrew said when he walked in. He worked tirelessly during the campaign, going door-to-door in his hilly, well-to-do adoptive neighborhood, and finally hitting upon *Roe* v. *Wade* as the ultimate deal-breaker for the undecided. "Okay," he'd say. "I understand that you're not crazy about either candidate. But just think of it this way: if Bush gets elected, he'll be the one to nominate the justice to that all-important seat on the Supreme Court that could potentially overturn *Roe* and take away a woman's right to choose. Do you really want to be responsible for that?"

He convinced *one* person not to vote for Bush.

One day he was in the car with Fanny; they were coming back from Gelson's. "Look at that," said Fanny, pointing to the neatly manicured lawn of a sort of prissy-looking little house that was probably worth $1.5 million. There was a sign planted right smack in the middle of the lawn. It said, simply, BUSH.

"That's so stupid," said Fanny, "to have a sign that says 'Bush.' You'd think in a neighborhood like this they could afford an actual bush."

"You know, Mom, why don't you come and do some work for the campaign too? You used to be so politically active."

"I'm too busy, between work and all the stuff I have to do at home," said Fanny. She was still working four mornings a week.

"Okay, feeding Otto, making dinner, playing solitaire. What else?"

"I'd do it if I weren't working," said Fanny.

Andrew was silent. He couldn't understand why Fanny was wasting her life.

"But I'll tell you one thing," said Fanny. "If Bush wins the election, I'm leaving the country."

Little Mike, in the meantime, had determined to make something of himself. He and Carmen lived in a thin-walled apartment on Moorpark Drive (which, Little Mike was fond of pointing out, spelled "Krap Room" backward), in a postwar building whose flimsy carports would collapse in the 1994 earthquake, crushing all the cars beneath, though fortunately neither Carmen nor Little Mike would be living there by that time, which was still way off in the future. Carmen got dressed up every day and jumped into her dull green '77 Toyota (which she'd bought to replace her Volkswagen; her father's used BMW had somehow never made its way into her life) at the respectable hour of 8:45 in the morning to go downtown to her job in the clothing mart. Little Mike was long gone by that hour, provided, of course, he could pull himself out of his heavy heavy alcohol-and-pot-induced sleep and drive, zombielike, to the phone room, where he was now office manager. Carmen, on the other hand, did not drink, and what usually would happen was the clock radio would go off with its terrible static buzz when the room was still pitch-black, at five in the morning, and Little Mike wouldn't even budge. It fell, therefore, to Carmen to wake him up and turn off the clock radio; soon she tired of the effort, and simply shook him once and turned off the alarm. If he didn't get up then, it was his fault, and the phone would start ringing at a quarter to six, with his boss on the other end, wondering where the hell Little Mike was.

What was Little Mike doing at night? Not going to bed early, as would behoove him; no, he was in the habit of going night-skiing. Somewhere along the line, since his scraggly adolescence, Little Mike's build had become fairly athletic; he would play football on Saturday afternoons, and he was becoming an excellent skier. He took a lesson one night, and the instructor told him his carved turn was already the best he had seen from a non-competitive amateur. Little Mike's skiing friend was Rob, the boyfriend of Nikki, a friend of Carmen's from work. Nikki and

Rob were both over six feet tall and skinny, with long straight black hair, spiked on top. They looked like twins. Rob was bassist in a metal band, and he loved to ski. He'd come and pick up Little Mike in his Bronco, and they'd drink Rémy XO from little silver cups all the way across the Pearblossom Highway and up into the mountains; and sometimes he'd have cocaine.

It was great fun, but at some level just beneath consciousness, Little Mike felt like shit all the time. The feeling would occasionally seep and bubble up around the edges, especially on days after he had done a lot of drinking and snorting coke. Probably smoking his beloved Marlboro reds made it worse; and probably he'd ski better if he quit.

One day Andrew told him he had a substance-abuse problem. "You think I have a problem?" said Little Mike. "That's a laugh." But sometimes he wondered if he was becoming an alcoholic. And so what if he was—what was he supposed to do, stop drinking? And then what? The whole thing was inconceivable. As an experiment, he decided not to drink *at all* for a week.

On Saturday, he went to Fanny and Edward's; he and Andrew were going to make dinner. At noon, before Little Mike arrived, Edward bellowed, "Fanny, what are we having for dinner? I want to figure out what wine to have."

"Whatever you want, Edward," she said. "They haven't decided what we're having."

"But I have to know," he said. "When are they going to decide? It's already noon."

"I don't know," said Fanny. "Relax, will you? Breathe through your nose."

"Well," said Edward. "I just think it's ridiculous." He looked around, sort of crazily. "Andrew!" he yelled.

"He's working in his room," said Fanny. "Why don't you just pick the wine, and they'll make something to go with."

"That's stupid," said Edward.

"Okay," said Fanny. "It's stupid."

Little Mike walked in and proclaimed, "Crown roast of lamb" before Otto could jump on him. Otto was the fattest golden retriever Little Mike had ever seen. "Hi, fat guy," he said, rolling around on the dark red Persian carpet with him.

"Don't make fun of him; he has a thyroid problem," said Fanny.

"Don't slobber," Little Mike said to the dog.

Edward selected two bottles of 1980 Dunn Howell Mountain cabernet from his wine locker and placed them on the sideboard, the highly polished walnut piece that had replaced the green thing. He might have a lot to criticize Little Mike for, but at least he could appreciate a fine bottle of wine.

"Guess what," said Little Mike as he took off his jacket, grinning. Fanny expected him to say he had gotten Raiders tickets for tomorrow. "I got a job as a *saucier*. I start next Tuesday, at L'Escoffier."

Everybody was stunned.

"How did you get a job like that?" said Andrew.

"I lied," he said. "Well, actually, I'm not going to start as the *saucier*; I'm going to start doing prep, just for a couple of weeks, and then they'll move me up."

Everyone agreed this was fantastic, and everyone was hoping the same thing; that maybe this would turn Little Mike around.

Now, what's your job going to be exactly?" said Edward later, when Little Mike and Andrew were cooking. Little Mike had refrained from pouring himself the glass of the Macallan eighteen-year-old single-malt scotch that he always had at Fanny's before dinner, and he really felt like having it now. But he didn't.

"*Saucier*," said Little Mike. "It's the guy who makes all the—"

"*I* know what a *saucier* is," said Edward. "What do you think I am, an idiot?"

"Edward," said Little Mike, "what's wrong with you? You're like a heart attack waiting to happen."

Little Mike went back to caramelizing his onions and thought about how life would be when he was a chef, which he felt would be sooner rather than later.

As everyone was sitting down to dinner, Edward started around the table pouring wine. "Carmen?" he said, when he got to her. "You should try this; it's really fabulous." He knew she didn't usually drink, but this was such a special wine.

"I'll taste it," she said. "Just a half a glass."

He poured hers, then came toward Little Mike with the bottle. Though he hadn't planned on having any, Little Mike realized at this moment that if he refused a 1980 Dunn, it would be making a more hugely big deal about the whole issue than he wanted. He decided just to sip it, in moderation. The wine went into the glass.

After he dropped Carmen off at home that night, he went out again, to his favorite local bar, The Fiddlers Three. When the phone woke him up the next morning, he had absolutely no recollection of how he had gotten home.

Home Stretch

And so it went.

By November of 1990, things were going so well for Edward that Fanny was able to quit her job by the time her birthday rolled around. She spent her time sitting at the kitchen table playing solitaire, looking out the window every now and again for deer on the hillside, or sitting on a chaise longue outside when it was warm, which was less often than it had been in the valley (this was the only thing she didn't like about the Westside, that it wasn't hot like the valley), reading fat paperbacks with titles like *The Boris Conundrum.*

George Bush was two years into his term as president, and Fanny was still a resident of the United States.

Andrew had moved out for a while when he was assistant-editing a series of music videos and gotten his own apartment; but that work dried up, he was broke, and he had once again moved back in. He was halfway through a screenplay, though he wasn't thrilled with it.

Little Mike's ascent into the culinary world looked more like a downward spiral. Aided by his charismatic charm and emerging technical mastery (though secretly he felt Andrew was a more imaginative cook than he), he talked his way into prominent positions in the kitchens of the best restaurants in town, which he inevitably lost after a few months. Arguments raged behind his back in the family as to whether he indeed lost jobs, as he said, because of personality conflicts with impossible chefs, or whether it might perhaps, as Andrew believed, be a case of his alcohol problem getting in the way. "Do you think he'd tell us," Andrew would say, "if he didn't show up because he was hungover?" He hated even to talk about it with Edward around, though, since Edward believed that alcoholism was simply a lack of willpower. Little Mike was weak, he argued. All he had to do was decide not to drink—which after all wasn't so very complicated, was it?— and that would be the end of the problem. Meanwhile, Carmen had left him in February, after he went night-skiing on Valentine's Day and then forgot her birthday; and she was tired of cleaning up after his messes, literally and figuratively. She didn't want to be married to an alcoholic, though she spared his family mention of any of this. Soon she moved in with her new boyfriend, an ex-friend of Little Mike's whom she'd started seeing when things were falling apart and he was always away on ski trips.

"You're moving in with the garbageman?" said Little Mike.

"He's not a garbageman," said Carmen.

"He collects junk, doesn't he?"

"He collects props," said Carmen, for her new boyfriend was a property master on the Warner Bros. lot in Burbank. She still loved Little Mike, and every time she thought about any piece of the whole thing, she became terribly sad.

264 ♦ LESLIE BRENNER

Fanny blamed Carmen for the breakup, which broke Carmen's heart even more, since Carmen felt closer to Fanny than her own mother, and now she was being disowned. How could Carmen of all people, Fanny asked herself, have an affair? When Andrew pointed out that it was Little Mike's alcoholism that broke them up, not Carmen's going out a few times with the garbageman, she knew at some level that Andrew was probably right, but she couldn't bear to think about it. What did all this say about her as a mother? Two of the brightest kids she had ever seen in her life—certainly they were both a hundred times brighter and more talented than any of her friends' kids—and one was dragged down by addiction, the other perpetually underemployed and living at home at the age of thirty. True, her friends' kids had boring jobs: one was an accountant, another a physical therapist, with a few small-time lawyers thrown in, and many of them were supported at least partially by their parents. But why must her kids flounder so? She had to believe that they were late bloomers—that Little Mike would get his drinking under control and become a famous chef, that Andrew would suddenly pull everything together and one day make brilliant films (she was surer of this prospect). But probably it was just the damn recession, and everything would be fine as soon as the country pulled out of it.

Act III

Alas, as the master Chekhov once said, introduce a blood transfusion in Act I and it had better result in the contraction of a terminal disease by Act III, and so Act III for Don meant a liver transplant, for he had been infected with hepatitis C. His fate was inescapable.

When he woke up from the seventeen-hour surgery, which was complicated by profuse bleeding from the considerable scar tissue left over from previous surgery, he saw his baby-faced surgeon through a fog, and then Valentina, and then he passed out again, sliding into a coma.

While Don lay comatose, Little Mike prayed for the first time in his life—he prayed that his father wouldn't die. He was pissed because the doctors had all said that the surgery was routine by now and that Don would wake up the next day and be perfectly fine, which wasn't the case at all.

Little Mike and Andrew would go to the hospital as often as they could bear it. However, they tried to time their visits not to coincide with those of Don's brother's second wife, Lois. Lois was a so-called therapist, and one who loved tragedy, at that. Andrew and Little Mike couldn't stand the way she would look at them with that heavy heavy look, acting like she was part of their family. Don had put up with her ever since Zachary had met her, though he always said she was a pain in the ass. So either Andrew or Little Mike, or both of them, would sit next to Don's bed in the intensive care unit, and watch him. Sometimes it looked as though his eyelids were fluttering a little, as if he were trying to open his eyes.

After three and a half weeks of this, Don came out of the coma. The first person he saw when he woke up was Lois. "I know I don't like you," he said when he came to, "but I don't remember why."

Part of Don's recovery, besides doing everything he could to get his body to accept his new liver, was to try to regain his memory, much of which he had lost. Over and over again, Andrew and Little Mike had to explain to him why he was in the hospital, and what the surgery had been. Then they'd move on to the current state of Don's life and the world. "You mean the Soviet Union doesn't *exist* anymore?" he said, incredulous, awestruck, stupefied, flabbergasted. "The Berlin *Wall* came down?" Little Mike brought him a small chunk of it, a triangle of cement, with red and green spray paint on one corner (a friend who was in Berlin just after the wall came down had brought it for him), to prove it to him. Nor did he remember that he had divorced Fanny. He remembered his phone number and street address in Van Nuys, even the address on Willoughby Street, the phone number of his office in Gateway East in Century City, his phone extension and his secretary's birthday, and even the terms of

Wayne Newton's first contract in Vegas. When he saw Valentina, he thought she looked vaguely familiar, but he had no idea she was his wife. He knew Andrew and Little Mike right away, but he didn't know where they lived or what their occupations were. In short, the past twenty-five years were a blur.

"Did your mom ever remarry?" Don said to Andrew one day from his hospital bed as he was trying to relearn his life, and Andrew said that she had married Edward. "Is he an okay guy?" said Don, scrunching up his face as if he vaguely remembered Edward, "or is he kind of an asshole?"

"He's okay," said Andrew.

"And the Beatles broke up," he reminded himself. "I can't believe that." (Andrew didn't have the heart to tell him that John was dead.) He lay in bed, looking up at the television, which was on but with the sound turned all the way down. He closed his eyes for a minute, and Andrew wondered if he were going to sleep. In a few moments he opened them again. "I'm trying to remember," said Don, "what's the connection between the Beatles and the Lakers?"

As Don grew stronger, and went home, and then weaker, and went back to the hospital, and stronger, et cetera, he thought a lot about the spiritual meaning of all of this, and even discussed it over lunch with his baby-faced surgeon, the thirty-nine-year-old chief of surgery at Cedars–Sinai Medical Center, to whom he felt he owed his life (though Little Mike and Andrew saw it differently). He was beginning to feel rather close to this young man, who in turn seemed to be fond of Don.

"You're a fighter," said the baby-faced surgeon. "That's what I really admire."

One day the surgeon had a heart attack and went through

triple-bypass surgery. And Don was visiting *him* in the hospital. This was during one of Don's strong periods, during which he was trying to rebuild his practically nonexistent law practice.

"You work too hard," said Don, and then something occurred to him. "You're playing God. That's a terrible responsibility you have, don't you see it?"

"I know," said the baby-faced surgeon. "I'm thinking of quitting. I'm not sure I can continue this way."

"What do you think you might do?" said Don.

"Well," said the surgeon. "I've been thinking. I might like to go into show business. Do you think you might be able to put me in contact with some people?"

Don beamed. This was a great idea. "As soon as you're better," he said, "we'll sit down and have lunch, and talk about it."

Manual Labor

It seemed Andrew's whole life was taken up with worrying about Don, who was still in and out of the hospital a year after the transplant, and worrying about Little Mike. He worried so much he could barely concentrate on his own life, which had become horribly stagnant, he hadn't noticed when. He thought of this as he washed a couple of big handfuls of fresh, grassy-smelling string beans in the colander, then began to snip off their ends with Fanny's kitchen shears. He'd make a salad of them tonight with shaved Parmesan and hazelnuts, the good olive oil, and maybe some aged balsamic vinegar.

Don, for all his faults, had been a good father. He must have been! He just slacked off when he hit his midlife crisis. At least that's what Andrew had always told himself. But much as Andrew racked his brain, he couldn't come up with any specific memory of Don being a great father.

In fact, Andrew was surprised to find that his memories of Don before he left were rather sparse. Maybe the notion that

Don was a good father was a myth. Part of the myth of the happy family.

Three or four string beans now remained at the wet bottom of the colander, and Andrew was about to toss them down the disposal. He always left a few vegetables at the bottom of the colander. Why? He couldn't help it. It felt pathological—as if no matter how much he wanted to trim every last bean, he couldn't.

From whence came this weird quirk?

Andrew forced himself to trim the last few string beans—which was actually physically painful—and then he rinsed out the colander, turned it upside down on the dish rack, tidied up, and turned off the light.

Aha. He knew what it was. For Don, fatherhood was a job left half done. Unfinished. In fact everything throughout Don's life had dangling ends. Andrew suspected, and rightly, that it was because Don had been orphaned.

It went even deeper than this, however. Don's mother, Gertrude, died in the middle of knitting a sweater, though she did wait until she finished the second sleeve. It was a navy blue lamb's-wool pullover for Don's brother, Zachary, who, incidentally, always got the better of two sweaters. Growing up, Don had never seen his parents complete anything. They didn't complete their children's upbringing—both had departed from the world by the time Zachary was eleven and Don was nine. Nor did they complete a life together. As Louellen would have said, it was a question of role models. As a result, in the Kelbow family, the dangling-ends problem was so pervasive it seemed to be genetic. Don always got the setups right, but never achieved the payoffs. He walked out on his marriage, and then on several perfectly good girlfriends. It didn't look as though he'd make it to see the births of any grandchildren; he'd never owned another house after the one in the valley with Fanny. He took up painting—for about a year; hiking, for three. In fact, Don was the consummate dilettante. Not only that, but he had aborted his fabulous career midstream in order to go out on his own. He had finally built up a successful practice, but had neglected—self-destructively?—to insure himself adequately, and was now hugely in debt to the hospital.

Poof! thought Andrew. I'm just like him.

Later, his cousin Amy called. Amy was a freelance advertising copywriter, specializing in direct mail, and a client of hers needed a writer for a word-processing manual. Andrew said he'd be happy to talk to the guy, who would call him the next day.

He went into the kitchen, where Fanny was playing solitaire. "Do you want to play a game of cribbage?" she said.

He took the cribbage board out of the drawer as Fanny scooped up her cards and started shuffling them. "I have an offer to write a word-processing manual for a thousand dollars," said Andrew as he placed little yellow and green pegs in the "start" portion of the board.

"That's great," said Fanny.

"Really? You think that's great? For what will probably be two months' work—"

"Okay," said Fanny. "That's terrible."

"Jesus Christ, Mom!" Andrew blew up. "What's wrong with you? Isn't there any middle ground? Can't we have an actual discussion about it?"

"Cut me some slack," said Fanny, "will you?"

"No," said Andrew. "Why? Why can't we have a real discussion about anything?"

Andrew wrote the manual, got the thousand bucks, did another in a month's time, this time for fifteen hundred bucks, and finally did what he should have done a long, long time ago, but had never had the nerve to even think about.

He moved all the way across the country, to New York, New York, on April 20, 1992.

"Hitler's birthday," pointed out Fanny, consigning it to the merely comical instead of what it was: heroic.

Coda

How sane the way the seasons marked the passage of time; to Andrew, it seemed too poetic to believe, too perfect. After ten days of cherry trees in riotous blossom, a warm promise of summer floated on the breeze. Petals fluttered down, giving way to tender leaves, and by mid-June Manhattan swelled in lush greenery. Cicadas buzzed through summer, and then August sizzled and steamed. They seemed overly appropriate, these seasons, as though each were a metaphor conjured up according to how one ought to feel that moment of the year. And then—and then: autumn in New York, even more crystalline and spectacular and winsome than the song.

Andrew blossomed, too, in New York. The moment he set foot on Manhattan soil, a screenplay started taking shape in his head—one about a young girl who leaves her home in the highlands of Oaxaca, Mexico, and lights out for a different life in the United States.

Andrew found a small apartment above a Caribbean restaurant

on West Twelfth Street in the Village, and the noise and the smells of rancid oil and coconut helped him work. He walked and walked, and worked and worked, crisscrossing the isle of Manhattan as he built characters and solved plot points in his head.

Three months later, he had raised twenty thousand dollars to start a shoestring production of his film. That was the first of many small successes that would eventually come his way.

He slept the deep and satisfying sleep of the creatively productive, sprawled out on his futon. But at 4:30 one morning in October he awoke, sitting up, thinking abruptly of Don. The phone rang a minute later. His father had died.

These tales always end in cremation, and naturally Don had wanted to pass into the next world by way of fire too. So Andrew knew not to be surprised by the weight of the ashes in the urn he held as he and Little Mike and Valentina sailed out on a cabin cruiser from Oxnard Marina to scatter them. The boat, an elaborate forty-foot affair with all kinds of radar and high-tech fishing gear, belonged to Valentina's father, Luco. He didn't talk much, and Andrew and Little Mike liked him for that. "I'll miss your dad" was all he said on the subject, for he had come to grow quite fond of his son-in-law.

It was October nineteenth, three days before Don's birthday. When the boat came close to one of the Channel Islands, Luco cut the motor. "Okay," he said. "I think this would be a good spot." Here, some miles out from shore, the water was startlingly clean and clear—nothing like the muddy surf of Southland beaches. Andrew thought about how his father disliked boats and things nautical; he was really more of a land-and-air person.

He had loved living near the beach because of the sea air. "He's even an air sign," pointed out Valentina. "Libra."

Don had wanted to be scattered from a plane, so he could be disbursed all over his beloved Los Angeles, but as it turned out, that was illegal in California. Valentina decided on the boat.

Andrew unscrewed the top of the brass urn and dumped the contents off the stern into the Pacific Ocean. The ashes made a solid gray cloud in the sea. The boat began drifting slowly away, and they watched the form as it undulated, phantomlike, in the cold black water.

On Don's birthday, there was a memorial service in Santa Monica. Little Mike was supposed to meet Andrew at Fanny's house at nine, since they were supposed to be at the synagogue an hour early. Fanny and Edward would go separately, arriving together for the eleven o'clock service. Andrew waited. And waited.

Little Mike showed up finally at 9:45, drunk.

This upset Andrew even more than losing Don had. He was so upset he couldn't speak.

Finally, on the way (with Andrew driving), he said, "How could you, Mike?"

"You've gotta be kidding," said Little Mike, fiddling with the radio. "You want me to go through this ordeal without a couple of shots?"

Andrew and Little Mike arrived as Valentina was talking with the rabbi, who seemed to have known Don quite well. "Oh, there you are," she said, and hugged them both. Andrew watched Valentina to see whether she noticed that Little Mike reeked of alcohol. Introductions were made.

The service began soon after, and the rabbi spoke of the spiritual side of Don. Andrew, in the front row, turned around to see the crowd. Don's brother, Zachary, was in the row behind him, with his wife, Lois, and daughters, Amy and Laurie. There was lovely Louellen, stunning in black, a lace mantilla wrapped around her shoulders. She really was her best at funerals. Louellen had called him at Fanny's just after he arrived to offer her sympathy. That's what came from being raised by the Bermans of Louisiana—she had the social grace to handle tragedy with aplomb. Valentina's family was there: Luco, Valentina's mother, her aunt, her daughters. Many of Don's old friends, friends of his and Fanny's.

Stan and Melissa were there, and Priscilla, who sat with Fanny and Edward. Fanny's mother Rose came too—she had flown out from New York with Andrew. Carmen was there, sans garbageman.

And scattered throughout were lots of show-business suits, agents and lawyers and producers—dealmakers all, witnessing the closing of the final deal. Andrew was surprised at how many people he didn't know.

Andrew got up and read the eulogy he had written on the plane, seated next to Rose. It had come flowing out of his pencil, and seemed to say all he felt about his father—the public side, anyway. Certain passages made the assembled laugh, and some wept as they laughed, and Andrew wept and read. When he stepped down from the podium, his ears felt hot. He wondered when it was really going to hit him that his father had died.

Now a crowd of ancient friends surrounded him, embracing him, and smiling and crying. Most of them hadn't seen Don in years. "He was one of a kind," said Stanley. "They broke the mold when they made him," agreed another.

A client of Don's, a well-known producer, stepped out from a pew to shake Andrew's hand and offer condolences. "I'll never forget the first time I met your dad," he said. "We were sitting on opposite sides of the negotiating table. Your father was such an unbelievably great negotiator that I said, 'Next time I want you on my side.' That's how he became my lawyer."

Up stepped Carmen, and she embraced Little Mike, and then Andrew. "That was beautiful, what you said," she told Andrew. She promised to ride with them to Valentina's, where there was to be a wake.

At Valentina's, the table was spread with deviled eggs, roast turkey, deli platter, breads. Fanny picked up a deviled egg, put it in her mouth. Rose, standing next to her, had shrunk with every passing year. "It's not right," she said quietly to Andrew and Little Mike. "My generation shouldn't outlive your parents. Your father was too young. And so much talent!"

Yes, thought Fanny. A talent for fucking up his life. Still, she was sad they wouldn't have him to kick around anymore.

And then, as if she were reading Fanny's mind, Rose turned around and faced her daughter, wagging a finger. "That man scrubbed the walls for you!" she said, and she started crying, trembling violently. Fanny put her arm around her and led her to a chair; Andrew offered her some lemonade.

"I'd prefer a small glass of scotch," she said. Little Mike went to the bar to get it, pouring himself one while he was at it. He was on his way to feeling maudlin.

For his part, Edward was more shaken by Don's death than

anyone would have expected. Only Fanny understood why: it forced him to face his own mortality.

Andrew boarded the plane two weeks later, having helped Valentina clear out Don's office and start to address the many problems of the diminished estate. Leaving wasn't easy—something that felt like a huge blob of inertia wanted to keep him there. Next time he came, after all, his father wouldn't be there.

Yet as the 727 made the ascent, executing its habitual slow U-turn over the Pacific Ocean and straightening out to the east, he felt that he could really go. And go. And go.

About the Author

LESLIE BRENNER, the author of the award-winning *American Appetite*, received an MFA in Creative Writing at Columbia University. Her book reviews and features have appeared in *The New York Times Book Review* and *Harper's*, among other publications. *Greetings from the Golden State* is her first novel.